RETURN TO PUCKERBRUSH

BY

C. DEANNE ROWE

Return to Puckerbrush
by C. Deanne Rowe

Published by Citrine Group, L.L.C.
Des Moines, IA

Cover by Sterling Design Studios

First Printing:

ISBN-10: 978-1-946122-27-8
ISBN-13/EAN-13: 978-1-946122-27-8

Printed in the United States of America

DEDICATION

Return to Puckerbrush is dedicated to all the readers of The Secrets of Puckerbrush who fell in love with the town and all the characters. Thank you for making Puckerbrush a success.

PROLOGUE

Glancing through a small opening in the tent cloth as he straightened the cuffs of his shirt, Edward Dalton smiled. The heat of the day had begun to give way to a cooler evening with a gentle breeze. The perfect conditions for bringing sinners to the Lord.

The creaking benches filled as the people gathered in the tent searched for seats. The crowd had been small the past few nights which meant the collection plates were almost empty. The members and people who attended those services must have spread the word through town bringing in more sinners to fill the collection plates.

Today was Wednesday and the townspeople normally attended church on this night so it was no surprise the tent was full tonight. Edward's ego teemed with gratification knowing the churches in town were missing many of their usual lambs.

The men were dressed in the freshly ironed shirts and pants brought out for attending church. The women wore dresses, some ill-fitting, which were also saved for church and special occasions. In small towns, your Sunday best was required only a few times. Everyone in attendance tonight must have felt this was one of those occasions. The air was thick with cheap aftershave and perfume.

Glancing through the crowd, Edward rated each woman's appearance, hoping there would be at least one prospect in tonight's crowd. So far, there was no one. All the women in attendance were with either a husband or suitor. The few possibilities were very young children who would not fill his specific needs: young, naïve, innocent, and attractive.

The crowd began to settle. Edward knew it was almost time for him to take the stage when from the corner of his eye he caught a glimpse of what would be his next triumph. She was beautiful. Her dress clung to each curve of her body, perfectly accentuating the woman she was becoming. She was alone. Edward could tell she was untouched by any man. Her innocence oozed from every inch of her body. She was perfect. She had to have been sent by God.

Edward watched as she took an empty seat on a front row bench in perfect view. He noticed her flawless posture as she crossed her legs at the ankles and tucked them under the edge of the bench. She brushed her hand over her dress to straighten any wrinkles. Taking a few seconds to enjoy what he was watching and mentally rehearsing his plan to gain her trust, Edward felt his pleasure rising. He had to clear his thoughts and rejoin reality. He had a sermon to give and a delicious lamb before him to fill the need the Lord had blessed him with.

****

"I pulled you from the crowd because the Lord spoke to me and told me you were in need of blessings." Edward sat down next to the young girl, careful not to get too close and scare her. He needed to gain her trust. Edward took her hand in his. She didn't pull back which was a good sign. He closed his eyes and prayed aloud "Lord, I have one of your lambs here with me. Please guide me to know what and how I'm to fulfill your blessing for this innocent child."

Edward opened his eyes to see tears running down the girl's face. He wiped them away and whispered. "Tell me your name."

"Mary." The girl's voice was breaking.

"What a beautiful name for a beautiful young girl." Edward knew he had to go slow or he would frighten her. "Can you tell me what's troubling you that the Lord feels you need to be blessed."

The young girl didn't answer for a few minutes. Edward could tell she was trying to decide how and what she felt she could share with him. He gave her the time she needed. There was no need to rush her. She had to come to him on her own. He had to build her trust.

"My mother died giving birth to me." Mary paused. "I feel like it was my fault she's dead. It's my fault my father's alone. It's my fault I've never known a mother's love."

Edward saw the opportunity he needed to move closer and comfort Mary as she began weeping. "Mary, Mary, Mary. It's not your fault your mother passed. It was her time. God may have taken your mother, but he let you live. If your mother would have been given the choice, she would have gladly let you live so you could experience life. A mother's love is so great she's willing to give her life to let her child live. You can't blame yourself."

"I don't know that. I've never had a mother to experience her love. I only know what my father has told me about her. He said she loved me, but I've never experienced her love." Mary explained. "I've no idea what a mother's love feels like."

"Maybe this is what the Lord is telling me." Edward put his arm around Mary's waist and pulled her close. "Maybe the Lord feels you need to experience a mother's love."

"How do I do that." Mary asked. "I'm not married. I don't have a boyfriend so marriage isn't in my near future."

Edward saw the questioning innocence in her eyes and he knew he had to go slow. The Lord had brought Mary to him, giving him the chance to give her a child so she would experience a mother's love. It was Edward's calling to make sure she gave birth to a child of God.

CHAPTER ONE

Berta stood in front of the group of regulars, all business owners in Puckerbrush, gathered at the largest of the Puckerbrush Café tables waiting as Martha moved around the table refilling everyone's iced tea glass or coffee mug.

"I'm so happy y'all managed to make it this morning. I think we've covered most of what was on the meeting agenda." Berta brushed back a strand of her grey hair that had fallen loose from her French knot as she glanced around the group. All the usual people were here, Beverly, Charles, Susan, and Frank. "I'm sorry Pam couldn't make it today."

Beverly Stanford held her hand up to be recognized. Her gold costume jewelry jingling on her wrist. "The baby isn't feeling well. I told her I would fill her in on what we talked about."

"Thanks for letting us know. I hope the baby feels better soon. Which one of you is taking care of her store if someone wants to buy some home décor? Do you need my help?" Berta glanced around the group.

"Pam asked me." Beverly waved her arm again, the jingling louder than before. "Susan's schedule's full with haircuts and perms and of course, Charles and Frank admitted they know nothing about decorating. They both said they would be no help at all. I'm right next door so I can slip over and leave my dress shop for a few minutes."

"Well, let me know if I can help you. I can make some time if I need to." Berta reached down on the table and picked up a magazine. "I have something I would like to share with all of y'all before we adjourn this week's meeting."

Martha placed the pitcher of tea and coffee carafe on the table and took a seat in one of the empty chairs at the table as John came jogging from the kitchen, cook's apron in one hand and running his other hand through his dark hair. He took the chair next to his mother. "Sorry I'm late."

"You're here now. That's all that matters." Berta smiled. "We've already discussed ideas about the possible increase in tourists due to our recognition in *Small-Town Living Magazine.* I think we've come up with some great ideas for souvenirs. Your mother can fill you in, John. Now, I would like to take a few minutes and read Abigail's article she wrote about our Puckerbrush Centennial Celebration. I'd have our Abigail read it to you but she and Matthew are in Chicago packing to move her here to Puckerbrush. We're gonna have a best-selling author living in Puckerbrush." Berta smiled and tried to clap her hands together as the rest of the group cheered.

"Not only is the article excellent, but there are some beautiful pictures of Puckerbrush which is the reason we'll be experiencing an increase in tourism to our sleepy little town. I have to say Abigail is as good a photographer as she is an author. I've given each of you a copy of the magazine if you want to follow along." Berta opened the magazine she was holding in one hand, grabbed the reading glasses hanging from the chain around her neck and placed them on her nose then cleared her throat and began.

Puckerbrush Texas celebrated its Centennial this year. If you have never heard of the small, quiet, southern town of Puckerbrush, let me fill you in.

When you first drive into Puckerbrush there's nothing spectacular for you to see. Traveling the road into town you'll pass farmland, cows and horses.

Eventually, you'll begin to notice the town. As you keep driving down the main road, you'll see older buildings lining Main Street. There's the Puckerbrush Café, the sheriff's office and fire station, and a few abandoned brick buildings which were once occupied by businesses that helped the farming families of Puckerbrush thrive.

What you won't see is the town's history which oozes from each brick in those buildings.

You won't see the hearts of the people who run the businesses and work hard to keep the town and its people safe.

You won't see the places in Puckerbrush that each of the townspeople call life changing. Special places which have helped to shape each person. The only way you'll know these places is to get to know the people.

I drove into Puckerbrush for the purpose of writing this article. I took the assignment for a friend who I now owe more than I can ever repay.

While researching Puckerbrush for my article, I met the most amazing people who I am proud to call family. Not just friends, but family. Small-town people don't get to know you, they welcome you with open arms into their town, their lives, their hearts. You become family. You can try to avoid it. You can try to stay distant. You can try to not become friendly and stay strictly business. It won't work.

People in Puckerbrush have a way of drawing you into their lives. They have a way of taking you under their wing. They have a way of knowing how to give you advice without you even know they're doing it. Before you become aware, you're welcomed and loved like you have never been before.

Martha is one of the strong, powerful women who live and work in Puckerbrush. She owns and operates the Puckerbrush Café with her son, John, and makes the most amazing apple pie. Martha and John don't wear uniforms because when you have dinner with them, they want you to feel like you're having dinner at home. You walk through the door, find your place at the table and will be served a delicious dinner you would think your mother or grandmother made. She serves everything from biscuits and gravy, to chicken fried steak, meatloaf, and perfect cheeseburgers and fries.

Berta is another of the strong, powerful woman who live and work in Puckerbrush. Berta owns and operates the comfortable and homey Puckerbush Motel which welcomes you as you drive into town. The outside of the Puckerbrush Motel is decorated with planters overflowing with beautiful flowers grown and cared for by Berta. She also shares her green thumb with the town by taking care of the planters lining the main street of town.

Both of these businesses began in Puckerbrush and were and are run by family. The town is kept safe by the well-qualified and caring Sheriff Matthew Thompson who, after attending college out of state, came back to Puckerbrush to keep the people he cares about safe.

These are just a few of the people who grew up in Puckerbrush and call it home. There are more people waiting to welcome you with open arms to their small, quiet town. All you have to do is plug the location into your GPS and enjoy the scenery. The best experience of your life is waiting for you.

Berta removed her reading glasses letting them fall against her blouse. She placed her copy of *Small-Town Living Magazine* on the table in front of her then took a seat. "I was so happy with this article. Our Abigail outdid herself. Not only did she write a wonderful article about our town, but she also included some amazing pictures."

"I agree." A huge smile crossed Martha's face which was framed by her short black hair. "Abigail has really become one of us. That makes me so happy."

"I know why it makes you so happy. You think you're going to be one of the first people to read her new books when they come out." John laughed.

"I'll be the first to admit you're right about that, John. I'm probably the biggest fan of Abigail's mysteries. Now I can say I'm friends with her. Or should I say friends with Leeza McBride?" Martha beamed with pride as she sat up straight and twisted in her seat.

"Don't forget she's just as big a fan of your apple pie." Berta leaned forward placing her arms on the table in front of her. "I think we should all think about who we want to play us in the movie that'll be made about Puckerbrush."

"I wouldn't get that far ahead of yourself, Berta." Martha laughed. "I'm going to frame the article and hang it on the wall of the café. I know just the spot. Right by the front door so everyone can read it when they visit." Martha pointed to the empty spot just waiting. "Don't you think that's perfect? There's plenty of light and everyone can see it right when they walk through the doors."

"Perfect." John agreed with his mother as he slipped his apron over his head.

"I'm going to find a place in the lobby of the motel for a framed copy also. I think it's a great idea." Berta clapped her hands together. "Maybe I'll get a small spotlight to shine on it so people won't miss it. I can't wait to see what it looks like."

"Do you think the article's going to bring a lot of people to Puckerbrush?" Beverly Stanford asked.

"I think so but I guess we'll have to wait and see. My understanding is *Small-Town Living Magazine* has a lot of readers. People who like to travel. There's potential for some of the subscribers to want to visit," Berta replied.

"It would be nice to have a full café. Everyone wanting a piece of my apple pie." Martha laughed.

"It would also be nice to have every room in the motel filled." Berta agreed. "I'm sure you wouldn't mind having a few more customers to your dress shop Beverly. Some more traffic in your hardware store, Frank, Charles, maybe some people will want to ship some of the souvenirs we sell home to themselves or friends and family. I'm sure Pam wouldn't mind having some more business in her home décor store." Berta noticed a smile on all the faces around the table.

"I'm going to go back into the kitchen and clean up from breakfast and get ready for lunch. You people can stay out here and dream." John laughed tying his apron as he made his way back toward the kitchen.

"You go ahead and laugh, John. I taught you better than that. Berta and I are right. You just wait and see." Martha turned her head to make sure John heard her.

John raised his hands in the air as if in surrender.

"I have to get back to the motel." Berta stood. "I put a sign on the door saying I would be back a half an hour ago."

"I need to go also." Beverly stood from her chair.

"I'll walk back with you." Charles smiled.

"Wait for me." Frank stood from his chair.

"I'll let you know who I find to frame my article. I'm sure Pam will know someone. Maybe we can do them at the same time." Martha waved to Berta as she walked out the café door. She carefully closed her copy of *Small-Town Living Magazine*. "You're going in a safe place."

She made her way toward the counter not really paying attention when the bells on the front door broke the silence of the café.

"Can we get a piece of your famous apple pie to go?"

Martha turned to see Matthew and Abigail walking through the café door.

"You're home!"

CHAPTER TWO

Martha held her arms out waiting for a hug from Abigail and Matthew.

"It's so good to see you both. How was your trip?"

"It was a long drive back. The weather is much nicer here than in Chicago." Matthew sighed as he stretched his arms in the air then ran a hand through his coal black hair.

"You really get to know someone when you travel a long distance together in the cab of a rental truck." Abigail glanced in Matthew's direction and smiled hoping he would return hers with one of those smiles she loved.

"She's right about that." Matthew shook his head as he hooked his sunglasses over the neck of his t-shirt. "Like how many stops you need to make after someone drinks a large soda."

Abigail slapped him on the arm, as she locked gazes with Matthew over the top of her sunglasses, squinting her brown eyes. "You didn't have to agree that quickly."

"I'm starving, Martha." Matthew quickly changed the subject. "Do you think you can get me one of your bacon cheeseburgers? The places where we stopped no way compared to your food."

"I would love one too, please." Abigail raised one of her fingers to be counted.

"Coming right up. Take your favorite seat by the window." Martha motioned toward one of the tables. "I'll bring out your burgers when they're done."

"It's so good to be home." Matthew slipped one of his muscular arms around Abigail's waist and led her to one of the favorite tables in front of the window.

"It is good to be home." Abigail agreed removing her sunglasses laying them on the table as she felt the tears fill her eyes. She fluffed her curly hair. "I don't think I've ever said that before and actually meant it."

Matthew hugged her before she sat down at the table. He smiled and took the chair next to her handing her one of the napkins lying on the table. "I should know by now to carry a supply of tissues with me."

"I've never been a crier. There's something about Puckerbrush and all the people I've gotten to know and love here. They've turned me into a crier." Abigail wiped her eyes as she looked across the street at the empty bench in front of the *Puckerbrush Newspaper* building. How she still missed seeing Eldon sitting there.

"We love you too." Matthew kissed her lightly. "You're one of the best things that's happened to Puckerbrush in a long time. You know we're going to have to tell everyone soon."

Just as she expected, Matthew always seemed to know how and when to change the subject to make her feel better. "I know. We can't make plans without someone finding out." Abigail held her left hand in the air admiring the ring Matthew had surprised her with.

"All right you two. Break it up. Your food's here." Martha laughed as she put both plates on the table in front of them. "It's so good to have you two back in Puckerbrush. Have you finish your next book yet, Leeza?" Martha placed her hands in the pocket of her slacks which showed off her slim figure, while she waited for Abigail's reply.

"I've been a little busy but I'm going to start working on it again as soon as I get settled. I promise." Abigail scrunched up her nose as she waited for Martha to tell her how she had been slacking and how she needed to get busy.

"I'm holding you to that." Martha pointed her finger at Abigail.

Abigail breathed a sigh of relief when she realized she wasn't going to receive a lecture. "Both you and my agent. She's been emailing and calling to make sure I'm still making progress."

"Does she know you're moving and settling here in Puckerbrush?" Martha asked.

"I've made sure she knows. She's cut me a little slack but not much. I promised her I would get busy as soon as I get here."

"If you need a place to write, you're always welcome here. I'll save you a table. Then I can say you wrote part of your book here in the Puckerbrush Café." Martha waved her hands around the dining room. "We would be famous for something other than my apple pie which you would have an endless supply of while you're writing."

"Thank you, Martha. I'll keep your offer in mind. There's something else I'm going to need your help with." Abigail glanced at Matthew and smiled.

"Sure. What's that?" Martha asked.

"Our wedding." Abigail held her left hand out and waited for Martha's reply.

"Wedding?" Martha screamed. "You two are getting married?" Martha wrapped her arms around each of them. "I'm so happy for you. You've no idea how happy."

"Thank you, Martha. You're the first person besides my parents who know." Abigail smiled.

"We need to have a party." Martha spread her arms in the air. "A huge party with everyone in Puckerbrush. It's not every day we have a wedding."

"Maybe not everyone in Puckerbrush." Matthew exclaimed. "Maybe just a small group. That would be a good way to tell everyone." Matthew smiled. "I like that idea."

"Matthew, you can't have a party and not invite everyone. Puckerbrush is too small to leave anyone out. We'll have it here in the café. I'll take care of everything. You two just have to show up." Martha clapped her hands together, smiling widely.

"If you plan to invite everyone, we need to make sure we invite Piper." Matthew insisted. "I want to make sure he's available to cover for me as sheriff when we go on our honeymoon. This time we were only gone four days so I didn't mind having one of the deputies fill in. We'll be gone almost two weeks for our honeymoon so I'd rather have Piper fill in if he can. They have enough deputies in Johnson County they should be able to do without him for that amount of time. I can get on his good side by inviting him."

"I'll do that. How's he doing? He hasn't been in for a while. It'll be good to see him. I'm sure John would like to see him also. If he covers for you while you two are gone, I'll get to see more of him." Martha smiled at the mention of catching up with Piper.

"I'm sure he'll be happy to see you and eat as much as your apple pie as he can while he's here." Matthew laughed. "You better start making pies now because you might not be able to keep up when he's in town."

"I can handle Piper just like I handle you and John. I love that guy. He might as well have been my son as much as he was around." Martha smiled. "I'll add him to the list."

"Thanks, Martha. I can't wait to meet him at the party. Matthew talks about him all the time. How they met at the academy." Abigail raised her finger in the air to make a point. "But we can't let you pay for everything. We'll be happy to pay for the food if you'll do the catering." Abigail insisted.

"We'll worry about that later." Martha waved her hand. "Right now, let's set a date. How about this Friday night?"

"Do you think we can keep our engagement a secret that long?" Abigail asked.

"You can try but you forget where you're going to be living. You can't keep anything a secret for more than an hour in Puckerbrush." Matthew laughed. "Did you forget?"

"You're right. Maybe we were in Chicago too long." Abigail smiled.

"Where are you going to stay while you're here?" Martha winked.

"I'm staying at Matthew's." Abigail smiled with a little hesitation in her voice. "I do need to find a place to store all my things. I hate to take over Matthew's house until we figure out where I'm going to set up an office."

"It doesn't look like you have much." Martha pointed out the window to the small truck Abigail and Matthew parked out front of the café. "I have a few empty rooms in the back of the café. You're welcome to store your things in one of them."

"You have rooms behind the kitchen?" Abigail asked.

"Of course. You remember, the Puckerbrush Café used to be the only hotel in town." Matthew mumbled with his mouth full of a bite of cheeseburger. "Martha can tell you all about it."

"My late husband's parents remodeled the kitchen, bathrooms and the dining area only. In the back of the café there are still some old rooms left from when this was the Puckerbrush Hotel." Martha motioned toward the back of the café.

"John uses one of the rooms now and then to nap when he's had a long day in the kitchen. They're still in good shape and some of them have the original furniture."

"That's amazing. I'd love to see them sometime. Are you sure you want to let me use one to store my things?" Abigail turned in her chair. She wanted to see the rooms. Knowing they were back there was piquing her curiosity.

"I'm sure. They're sitting pretty much empty except for the few things I have stored in there and John's stuff. You might as well use one of them." Martha shrugged.

"Thank you, Martha. I might take you up on that. I'll be happy to pay you something for using a room." Abigail smiled.

"I'll take anything you owe me in books." Martha pointed her finger at Abigail. "That means you need to get busy writing."

"I guess it does." Abigail's imagination started working. She couldn't wait to see the rooms.

"One way or another she's going to make sure you're writing." Matthew patted Abigail's shoulder. "Maybe you should finish your burger then we can go home, sort through what you want to keep at the house and bring the rest back here. The quicker we get you settled and back to writing, the happier Martha's going to be."

"That sounds like a perfect plan." Martha laughed. "I'll leave you two alone so you can finish your meal. Let me know if you need anything. We can talk about your wedding plans later."

Abigail watched as Martha bustled back toward the kitchen then turned to Matthew. "You two are going to be watching my every move, aren't you?"

"I shouldn't have to remind you it was your idea to move to Puckerbrush. Something about falling in love with the gorgeous sheriff."

There was the smile. One of the reasons Abigail had been drawn to Matthew to begin with. Placing her chin in her hand and taking a few minutes to enjoy the moment, she finally answered.

"I'm beginning to remember. It's all starting to come back to me now." Abigail leaned in and kissed him lightly. "Maybe we should finish our lunch. Then we can go home and you can help me remember a little bit more why I moved to Puckerbrush."

"It's a deal." Matthew grabbed his cheeseburger and took a large bite. With his mouth so full he could hardly talk he managed to mumble as he pointed to Abigail's plate. "Get busy."

CHAPTER THREE

"A little more this direction." Abigail waved her arms to her left doing her best to direct Matthew as he backed up the rental truck in the direction of the back door of the Puckerbrush Cafe. "Stop!" She held her hands up in the air.

Matthew climbed out of the cab as Abigail began unlocking the rolling back door of the rental truck.

"I'll go find Martha and see which one of the rooms we're going to store your things in." Matthew disappeared into the café.

Abigail climbed into the back of truck and began moving the boxes closer to the edge of the door of the truck. Matthew appeared in the café doorway motioning for her to follow him.

"Come take a look around. Martha said we could use any of the rooms. I want you to choose."

Abigail climbed down out of the truck with Matthew's help and followed him down the hallway of the café. There were two doorways along the way he had opened for her to look into. She walked into the first room. It looked as if the room was furnished out of some of the old westerns Abigail had watched with her grandmother. Floral design wallpaper covered the walls. Lacy beige curtains tied back to show sheers hanging from the window.

The bed was a double-size mattress covered with a handmade quilt on an iron bedframe. She reached down and pushed her hand up and down on the bed causing it to creak. Abigail imagined how noisy it would be to sleep on. A crystal chandelier hung above the bed. There was an old, wooden dresser with a ceramic bowl and pitcher sitting on top. One single night stand sat beside the bed adorned with an antique oil lamp.

"Martha wasn't kidding. This room has to have all the original furniture from when the hotel was built. This is amazing. It's like walking back in time. Does the other room look like this?" Abigail asked as she rubbed her hand over the furniture.

"The other room's more for storage. I think we should put your stuff in that room. There's no dust in here and it's really clean. This must be the room John uses now and then." Matthew laughed as Abigail was lost in thought. "I've seen that look in your eyes before. You have an idea for a book, don't you?"

"I do." Abigail walked around the room, touching everything as if she was soaking up the history hidden in the pieces of furniture.

"Maybe you should decide which room you want to use to store your things. You can always come back and finish whatever it is you're doing some other time." Matthew waved his hand in the air as he watched Abigail look around.

"You're right. Let's use the other room to store my things." Abigail reluctantly agreed. "I do like the way this room's talking to me though." Abigail continued running her hands across the tops of the furniture.

"I'll go get some of the boxes and start bringing them in. I can tell you aren't going to be a lot of help." Matthew disappeared down the hallway.

"I wonder if Martha would let me write in this room sometime. I can feel the words flowing. The feelings are so strong." Abigail continued looking around the room. She felt like a child in a toy store.

"Do you think you could store those words and feelings somewhere in your memory and come help me unload the truck?" Matthew asked as he walked by the doorway carrying a box from the truck.

Abigail took one last look around the room and then reluctantly joined Matthew.

****

After the truck was empty, Abigail returned to the first room to take one last look around. She closed her eyes and could see herself writing. Her fingers moving around the keyboard.

"We're all done." Matthew interrupted her thoughts. "Are you ready to go home?"

"I'm going to ask Martha if it would be all right if I came in here to write now and then. I probably need to ask John also." Abigail kept looking around the room exploring new things she would find. Some of the clothing lying around the room she could tell was John's.

"You're serious about that? I thought you would write at the house. Maybe sit out on the deck watching the wildlife." Matthew asked. "We also talked about you using Eldon's building for an office. It has all the reference material you'd need."

She shrugged. "I can do that. I've been thinking about other ideas for Eldon's building. It's just that I can feel the energy here in this room. The ideas are coming to me faster than I could write them down. I'm going to have to trust my memory."

Abigail moved closer to the single window in the room and pulled back the curtains taking in the view of the town. She could almost imagine the people who had stood in the same spot where she was standing taking in the same view. Her thoughts swirled. Was the person who rented this room hiding? Were they hiding or were they watching? What secrets were they hiding? She knew first-hand about the secrets Puckerbrush.

"I'm sure Martha wouldn't mind you writing in here now and then. You can ask her when we stop and tell her we have everything moved. I'll return the truck and then we can have some apple pie. I'd like to hear the other ideas you've got for Eldon's building." Matthew took Abigail's hand. "Are you ready?"

"I am." Abigail closed the curtains and turned toward Matthew. "I'd say after all the work we did; we earned some pie. I'm starving."

****

"We found room for everything. Thank you again for letting me store my things." Abigail gave Martha a quick hug. "They won't be there long. Matthew and I just have to sort out what we need and don't need. We moved me in such a hurry, I didn't have time to get rid of things before I packed. Most of it's for my office. I left the rest of the boxes at Matthew's."

"You don't need to hurry. Like I said, those rooms are unused except by John." Martha placed two slices of apple pie in to go boxes on the counter. "Where's Matthew?"

"He's returning the truck. He'll be back to pick me up when he's done." Abigail took a seat at the counter.

"Everyone I've invited is planning to come to your engagement party Friday night. It's going to be so much fun. I get to rub it in everyone's face that I was the first person in Puckerbrush to know about your engagement." Martha grinned.

"I really appreciate you doing this, Martha. Especially on such short notice. Two days doesn't give you much time."

"I'm happy to do this for you guys." Martha patted Abigail's hand. "When are we going to talk about your wedding plans?"

"I'll tell you what I've decided already. I want to have the wedding in Matthew's backyard. That's where we spent a lot of time when I was here in Puckerbrush. It has a special meaning for me. I think Matthew will feel a little like his parents are there also."

"That's a wonderful idea, Abigail. It'll be a beautiful wedding. Matthew's one lucky guy." Martha smiled.

"Thanks. Also, my parents are planning to be here and my Uncle Charles is coming with them to perform the ceremony. He made me promise when I was a little girl that he would be the one to perform my wedding. I just have to let them know when and they'll make the trip. I can't wait for them to meet all of you." Abigail felt it was only appropriate for all the people she loved to meet.

"I can't wait to meet them," Martha moved in closer. "Tell me, what did they think of Matthew?"

"They like him. A lot." Abigail eyes widened. "He made a very good impression on my father."

"How's that?" Martha asked, leaning against the counter with her arms crossed.

"My parents flew into Chicago to meet Matthew while we were there packing. I guess he'd been planning how to ask my father for my hand in marriage before we left for Chicago. He had the ring already. He just needed my father to approve." Abigail's eyes began filling with tears.

"That sounds like my Matthew." Martha smiled and nodded with approval.

"My father was very impressed to say the least. How could he say no? Anyway, we all went out to dinner after Matthew talked to my father and he proposed in front of them. It was very romantic."

"It sounds like it was perfect. I'm so happy for you two. I know I've told you that only a few hundred times, but it doesn't hurt to make sure." Martha smiled.

"What are you two talking about?" Matthew asked as he walked through the café door.

"Our wedding." Abigail stood up from her seat and gave Matthew a hug.

"Knowing you two you probably have it all planned." Matthew took a seat at the counter next to Abigail.

"Not quite. There are still a few details to work out. Like asking Berta to help with the flowers. With her green thumb, she would be perfect." Abigail glanced at Martha for her approval.

"Oh, that's perfect!" Martha exclaimed. "We can ask her Friday night. She's making the table arrangement for your engagement party. I'm sure Berta would be happy to help you out. She knows her flowers."

"I was right. You two will make our wedding perfect. I can just leave everything up to you." Matthew laughed.

"There's no way you're getting out of helping." Martha pointed her finger at Matthew. "I'm sure we can think of plenty of things for you to take care of."

Matthew leaned over and kissed Abigail's cheek. "I'll do anything to make our wedding day perfect."

Abigail smiled and leaned her head on his shoulder. "Thank you. No matter what, our wedding will be perfect."

"You two are so cute!" Martha smiled. "I know you're going to have beautiful children."

"Let's order something to eat. I'm starving." Matthew patted Abigail on the knee.

"You already have pie." Abigail pointed to the slices of pie Martha had placed on the counter.

"I know, but I worked up an appetite moving all those boxes." Matthew rubbed his stomach.

"Sounds good to me," Abigail replied.

"Way to avoid the subject of children." Martha laughed as she handed the two of them a menu.

Matthew winked at Abigail and smiled. She knew Martha was right. They were going to have beautiful children, especially if they had Matthew's smile.

CHAPTER FOUR

Tapping a spoon lightly against her glass of wine, Martha spoke up. "Can I have everyone's attention."

Abigail glanced around the decorated café as everyone finished talking and looked in Martha's direction. The tables were covered with white linen clothes. The food table was adorned with silver trays holding appetizers, glass goblets for wine, and of course, beautiful floral centerpieces surrounded by silver candleholders. Martha, John, and Berta had gone all out for them. Her heart was full.

"As I told y'all when I invited you here tonight, we're welcoming the newest resident of Puckerbrush, Abigail Stratford."

Abigail could feel the love in the room as everyone applauded and Matthew placed his arm around her waist pulling her close. She nodded and smiled in appreciation.

"What I didn't tell all of you..." Martha paused as she glanced at Abigail. "Is that Abigail and Matthew have an announcement." She motioned in their direction.

Abigail looked at Matthew and then turned toward the crowd. "I'm so happy to call Puckerbrush home now. I'm so happy that I'll be able to see all of you every day. Matthew and I do have some news though. While we were packing my things in Chicago, Matthew asked me to marry him." Abigail had to pause while the room erupted in cheers. When the room quietened, she continued. "Of course, I said yes."

"We're so happy for you." Berta clapped her hands together as a huge smile filled her face.

"I hope everyone has something to drink because I think we should toast the couple." Martha held her wineglass in the air and waited for everyone to do the same. "To the happy couple. We wish you nothing but happiness in your future together."

Matthew kissed Abigail to the sound of the room filled with glasses clinking together and congratulations echoing through the café.

"Help yourself to food and drinks. This party is meant for all of us to have fun and socialize. I want everyone to make sure they do so." Martha winked at Abigail and then began walking around the food table checking all the serving dishes.

"Piper." Matthew called out.

A handsome man around Matthew's age began walking toward them. Abigail was amazed at the similarity in features between him and Matthew. They had the same color of hair and the same dark eyes. Even his smile was familiar. It didn't give off the same electricity as Matthew's but it was close.

"You must be Abigail." Piper held his hand out for her to shake.

"You must be Piper." Abigail smiled. "I've heard so much about you."

"I hope whatever you heard was good." Piper reached over and gave Matthew a quick man hug. "It's good to see you. It's been too long."

"I agree." Matthew pulled Abigail close. "I'm happy you got a chance to meet Abigail."

"Me too. Matthew told me all about you. I understand you're a mystery author." Piper looked at Abigail.

"I am."

"Would I know anything you've written?" Piper asked.

"I write under the pen name of Leeza McBride."

"Really? I've read your books then. They're great." Piper said. "I've never known an author."

"Did you read her article in *Small-Town Living Magazine*?" Matthew asked.

"I haven't yet. I've been meaning to find a copy in the bookstore but I haven't yet." Piper said.

"Let me know if you don't find one. I'll send you one of the copies I have." Abigail offered.

"That would be great." Piper glanced around the room. "I'm going to let you guys talk with some of the other guests while I go give Martha and John a hard time. I haven't seen them in a long time either. Congratulations on your engagement. I'm happy for you both. We'll talk again before I leave." Piper smiled.

"That means you're going to be available to cover for me when we go on our honeymoon, right?" Matthew asked.

"You let me know when, and I'll put it on my calendar." Piper patted Matthew's shoulder. "I'm going to go get a piece of Martha's apple pie."

Abigail watched as Piper walked up behind Martha and gave her a bear hug making her let out a squeal. "He seems really nice."

"Piper? He's a great guy," Matthew replied.

"And you said you two met in the academy?"

"Yes. I'd come back to Puckerbrush after college and Piper decided he wanted to make public service his career. I'd lost my parents about a year before we met and he'd just lost his mother. We helped each other through a lot of stuff most guys don't know how to handle. After we completed the academy, we'd get together along with John, hang out and have a few beers."

"Has anyone ever told you two that you look alike?" Abigail asked.

"I know Piper's father told us he was always asked if I was his son because Piper and I resembled each other. Other than Piper's father, I don't think anyone else has mentioned it." Matthew shrugged.

"Amazing." Abigail murmured.

"I see that writer brain of yours going to work. Put Leeza away and let's enjoy our engagement party without her hanging around." Matthew laughed.

"You know by now, I can't just turn her off. When she gets an idea in her head, she won't let it go." Abigail looked at Matthew's expression. "I promise I'll try."

"That's all I ask." Matthew kissed her on the forehead. "Let's get something to eat before Piper eats it all."

CHAPTER FIVE

"Your engagement party last night was so much fun." Martha beamed. "It was a great reason for a Friday night celebration. We both know Puckerbrush needs more of those. I'm so glad everyone was able to make it. Especially Piper. We didn't give everyone much notice."

"I loved meeting Piper. He was as nice as Matthew said. It was fun and being able to surprise everyone with our engagement was fun also. I can't believe you got them here without telling them why." Abigail laughed. "Berta didn't even question why you wanted flowers for all the tables."

"Oh, that was easy." Martha waved her hand through the air. "I told her I wanted to spruce up the café for all the new customers we've been having come through."

"Great idea." Abigail smiled.

"I've lived in Puckerbrush for a long time. I've learned a few secrets of how to pull things off without anyone finding out." Martha winked at Abigail. "Maybe someday I'll pass those secrets down to you."

"I would love that." Abigail clapped her hands together. "It's so hard to keep a secret here."

"My mother always said she would know if we did anything wrong before we did it and she was right." Martha laughed.

"I also wanted to tell you how much I appreciate you letting me use one of the back rooms. I've gotten so much writing done on my new book." Abigail watched Martha as she put another pot of coffee on to brew.

"As long as you're writing, I'm happy." Martha took a cloth and started wiping off the counter. "Having you here's a pleasure. I wish you didn't feel like you have to help me out around the restaurant. I told you a copy of your book would be payment enough."

"I know what you said but business has picked up since my article in *Small-Town Living Magazine* was published. You've been working a lot harder and a lot more hours. Helping you out during lunch is the least I can do." Abigail insisted.

"Both John and I have been putting in more hours. The tourist business certainly has picked up since your article. I have to admit you're a good waitress though. You really help out." Martha patted Abigail's hand.

"I've worked my share of jobs in restaurants. Waitressing is how I supported myself until my books took off. I worked just about any type of job I could find to help pay the bills." Abigail liked helping Martha and John. She didn't remember having as much fun when she was working to pay the bills.

"I'm glad you decided to use one of the back rooms to write but I was sure you were going to set up an office in Eldon's building. After all everything in the way of reference material is stored in that building," Martha replied.

"I debated it but I think I have a better idea for that building." Abigail gathered her thoughts before mentioning them to Martha.

"What kind of idea? I hate to see that building sit empty." Martha pointed across the street to the old *Puckerbrush Newspaper* building. "I don't think that's what Eldon would have wanted."

"What if it was turned into a museum?"

Martha's reply came quicker than she expected.

"That's a wonderful idea, Abigail." Martha stopped what she was doing and stared across the street. "I mean Eldon took such good care of all the reference material and all the newspapers. He kept a detailed log. It's like a library and we could add some Puckerbrush souvenirs to sell to the tourists. Maybe some t-shirts and some hats. Oh, and some of your books. You could sign some of your books and we could make them available." Martha's face lit up.

"We'll have to see about the books." Abigail paused. "I want this to be a tribute to Eldon. He certainly did take care of everything in that building. He knew right where everything was. I've been thinking if it was turned into a museum the schools could use it to teach the local children about Puckerbrush. There's so much history in there. It would be a great learning experience." Abigail watched for Martha's expression to change.

"You're right about that." Martha agreed, nodding enthusiastically. "Plus, opening it up to tourists is a great idea. It would give them somewhere to go while they're here."

"That's perfect." Abigail smiled. "I have another idea to run by you also. What if we ask Berta to head the committee to collect donations and maybe do some decorating? It would be right up her alley."

"Oh, lordy yes. I love that. Berta's the perfect person." Martha smiled. "Let's call her."

"Let's do." Abigail searched her pocket for her cell phone but was interrupted by the ringing of the bell on the café door. A striking, young woman walked through the doorway looking around the café as if she was in unfamiliar surroundings. She took her time studying the photos hanging on the wall. Abigail remembered her first visit to the café and how she was taken in by all the photos.

"Hi." Abigail poured a glass of water from the pitcher on the counter and slowly moved in the direction of the woman. "Welcome to Puckerbrush Café. You can take a seat anywhere. I'll get you a menu."

The young woman looked around the café and picked one of the empty tables along the wall. As Abigail placed a menu and the glass of water in front of her she tried to make conversation thinking it would make the woman feel a little more comfortable.

"I'm Abigail. Take your time looking through the menu. Anything you decide on will be good. I'll be back to take your order." Abigail started to walk away until the young woman stopped her.

"There is something you can help me with." The woman brushed a strand of her straight black hair out of her eyes.

"What's that?" Abigail asked.

"I'm looking for someone who lives here in Puckerbrush. His name is Matthew Thompson. Do you know him?"

Silence took over the room as Abigail tried to decide how she was going to answer the woman's question, while wondering her reason for asking.

"I do know him." Abigail paused. "How do you know Matthew?"

"I'm sorry. I'd really like to talk with Matthew if you could tell me where I could find him." The woman was polite but firm. The look on her face told Abigail she wasn't going to get very much information questioning her.

"Let me call him and have him come here to talk to you if that's all right. He's just down the street." Abigail pointed in the direction of the sheriff's office. "In the meantime, if you would like something while you wait, I can take your order. Martha's apple pie is the best."

"I'll take a piece of apple pie and a glass of iced tea, please." The woman handed the menu back to Abigail. "How long will it take for Matthew to get here?"

"It won't take long at all. I'll go call him and get your pie and tea." Abigail picked up the menu off the table and walked back toward the counter to find her cell phone.

"Hi, it's me. You need to drop everything and come to the café. There's someone here who wants to talk to you." Abigail ended her call. Her thoughts were going places she wasn't sure she wanted them to go.

****

Abigail greeted Matthew with a hug when he walked through the front door of Puckerbrush Café.

"She's right over there." Abigail pointed to the table where the young woman was sitting. "I tried to ask her what it is she wanted but she said she wanted to talk to you."

He glanced over at the table before taking Abigail's hand. "Let's go see what she wants."

"She told me she only wanted to talk to you. I think maybe I should wait over here while you talk to her. I don't want to make her uncomfortable." Abigail placed her free hand on Matthew's arm and pushed him toward the table.

"I don't know her and I don't know what she wants. If she wants to talk to me, you can hear whatever it is she has to say." Matthew pulled Abigail with him as he made his way toward the young woman's table.

"Are you Matthew Thompson?" The young woman stood and smiled extending her hand for Matthew to shake. "I'm Emily. Emily Clayton. I emailed you letting you know I think we might be related."

CHAPTER SIX

Abigail tried to keep her eyes from bugging out. She shifted her glance between Matthew and the young woman. There was some resemblance. Her dark eyes, her chin and the color of her hair were similar to his.

"Take a seat. It looks like we have some things to talk about." Matthew pointed to the table where the woman had been sitting. "I see you've already learned about Martha's apple pie."

"I have and it's very good." Emily sat down in her chair.

"I'll get you a glass of tea, Matthew and a refill for you, Emily." Abigail turned and walked toward the counter.

Martha waited for Abigail to walk behind the counter before she moved close and whispered. "What does she want? Did she say?"

"She said she thinks she and Matthew are related."

"What?" Martha's mouth was wide open.

"I know exactly how you feel."

Abigail knew the look on Martha's face was the same one she had when Emily introduced herself and matched the feeling she had in the pit of her stomach. How did she find Matthew? How did she get his email? Why hadn't he said anything to her? She had so many questions that she knew were going to have to wait.

Picking up an empty glass and the pitcher of iced tea behind her, Abigail made her way back to the table trying to pick up any of their conversation she could. It must be going all right because both of them where smiling.

"Here you go." Abigail placed a glass in front of Matthew and filled it with tea and then refilled Emily's glass already on the table.

Matthew reached out and took Abigail's hand.

"I want you two to meet. Abigail, this is Emily Clayton. Emily, this is Abigail Stratford."

"It's nice to meet you, Abigail." Emily smiled.

"You too, Emily."

"Emily found me on the website I had signed up on for DNA testing." Matthew explained.

"When did you do that?" Abigail was surprised and a little disappointed he hadn't mentioned anything to her.

"Shortly after I found out about my past. It was around the same time you went back to Chicago the first time. Along with reading the journals, I realized I needed to find out everything I could about where I came from. Doing DNA testing was the easiest and most logical way." Matthew explained.

"I'm happy you took that step. You realize what you find out is only genetic. It doesn't change anything about the people here in Puckerbrush. They're all still your family." Abigail squeezed Matthew's hand.

He smiled up at her. "I know that. I realized I knew nothing about my father's side of the family. I needed to know where they came from, if there were any health issues I needed to know about, and most important, if I had any relatives I needed to know about. I guess it turns out I do." Mathew glanced at Emily.

"So how are you two related?" Abigail asked.

"We're cousins, I guess." Emily paused for a minute letting that information sink in. The look of surprise on Abigail's face must have caused her to hesitate.

"The reason I started looking is my mother has been diagnosed with Alzheimer's. She was adopted so I wanted to help her try and find the medical history of her biological family. She'd never had a desire to find out her background so I had to." Emily took a drink of her tea and then continued.

"Anyway, I hadn't found a match who would acknowledge my request to email and connect with them. Matthew was the only one who allowed contact. He was close enough to visit so I decided I would try. My mother and Matthew's father have the same biological father." Emily put her hands on the table, lacing her fingers and waited for a response from Matthew or Abigail.

"You mean the traveling evangelist?" Abigail asked.

"It sounds like you know about him." Emily smiled at Abigail.

Abigail shifted her gaze to Matthew and back to Emily before replying. "I know of him, but not much about him."

"Amazing huh? It seems the preacher got around." Matthew pulled the chair next to him away from the table for Abigail to sit down.

"What do you mean?" Abigail took a seat in the chair.

"It seems our biological grandfather made a habit of fathering children in the places he would stop and hold revivals." Matthew leaned back in his chair, his mouth a tight line.

"How many children are we talking?" Abigail glanced back and forth between Emily and Matthew waiting for an answer.

"At last count, I've found five matches who are biological brothers and sisters for my mother."

"Five!" Abigail exclaimed.

"Those are only the ones who've submitted DNA." Emily explained. "Who knows how many haven't. It also seems all five were born within a few years of each other. Their birthdates range from the late nineteen fifties to early nineteen sixties."

That's about right. My father was born in sixty-two," Matthew replied.

"How many have you contacted?" Abigail asked.

"Now that I've met Matthew, he makes three," Emily held three fingers in the air. "I've tried to get the other two to meet with me but they haven't responded. Matthew's the only one who even answered my email."

"Did you explain you were searching for medical reasons?" Matthew asked.

"Yes. I tried everything I could think of, but I never received a response from any of them. I know it won't help my mother now that she has been diagnosed, but I wanted to find out which parent's family had the gene." Emily explained.

"Have you found anyone on your mother's paternal side? Did she have any siblings on that side of her family?" Matthew sat up in his chair waiting for Emily's reply.

"She did. Her biological mother had two more children. I found the gene came from her mother's side of the family. There have been several relatives diagnosed with Alzheimer's including her biological mother." Emily explained.

"It doesn't come from our grandfather's family?" Matthew asked as he released an audible sigh.

"I don't believe so, but there's always the possibility both families have the gene. I don't know for sure. When I found out how many siblings there were on her biological father's side, it became more of a search for the truth than for medical information." Emily took another sip of her tea.

"Since you're a sheriff, can you find out anything more about these people? Maybe help locate them?" Abigail turned to Matthew and asked.

"I'm not sure. I'd need their names at least," Matthew explained.

"That's a problem. I can't even get their names without their permission to share. I've no idea who they are." Emily sat back in her chair and rubbed the back of her neck. "You're the only one who would give me any information."

"Why don't I go get you two something to eat. I think you're going to be here for a while." Abigail stood up next to the table. "Besides I'm sure Martha's dying to know what you two are talking about. I better go fill her in before she decides to come join us at the table."

Matthew turned and motioned for Martha to join them. He couldn't help but laugh at how fast Martha moved from behind the counter and made her way to the table. "Now the party's complete." Matthew laughed.

Abigail felt for her cell phone in her pocket and then remembered she had left it on the counter.

"I'll be right back. You guys fill Martha in." Abigail found her cell, picked it up and dialed. "Hi, Sam. It's Abigail. I have a favor to ask."

CHAPTER SEVEN

"Wow! That's some story," Sam replied. "I don't really know what to say."

"Say you'll help me out." Abigail begged. "Do you think you could run an article? I have to get Matthew to agree before we do. I want to find a way to help him out. Help him find the family he didn't know he had."

"I think it's a great idea for the right magazine. I'm not so sure about *Small-Town Living*. I can call in a few favors I'm owed and see if I can find the right platform for your story. I've run some ads for other magazines that might be interested, but how do you know the right people will read it?" Sam asked.

"I'm hoping with all your, Katie's and my connections, the right people will and maybe it'll get picked up nationally. If that happens, the better the chances someone connected to Matthew will read the story."

"I'll do what I can, Abigail. I can't promise you anything. You know that, don't you?" Sam said.

"I have to take that chance, Sam. You know me. I never back down from a challenge." Abigail reminded him.

"I've known you long enough to realize I should've thought before I spoke."

Abigail could hear Sam laughing on the other end of the phone.

"I'm going to call in all the favors I can for interviews. Maybe I can get some television spots. The more we do, the more people will see. I'm hoping that if we find just a few people who know their family history, we'll find the other people we're looking for."

"I wish you all the luck you need, Abigail. Katie and I will do whatever we can to help."

"I know, Sam. I'll let you know what Matthew says and when I have the article written. Thank you and Katie so much."

Abigail ended her call, took a deep breath and headed back to the table where Matthew and Emily were sitting.

"I have an idea. It'll depend on if you two are willing to tell your story. If you are, we might be able to find some of the people you're looking for." Abigail glanced at Matthew hoping that what she was asking wouldn't send him backward.

"I've been trying to come up with any idea and I've had no luck. I'd like to hear what idea you have." Emily explained.

"Tell us what you're thinking and we'll let you know." Matthew sat back in his chair.

"Okay." Abigail moved closer to the table. "I have a friend, Sam, who's a magazine editor."

****

"What do you think? Are you willing to take a chance?"

Abigail was even more excited about her idea now. Going through it with Matthew and Emily had helped her work through the details a little more. She knew she could get some publicity. Now it was whether Matthew and Emily wanted to share their story with the world. It had taken Matthew several months to even want to talk about his past. Sharing it with the world might set him back. Their wedding was coming up soon. Abigail knew it would be difficult for Matthew to enjoy the day if he wasn't in the present.

"I'd be willing to talk to whoever will listen." Emily nodded. "What about you Matthew?"

Abigail took Matthew's hand, looking him directly in the eye. "I know how hard this has been for you. I don't what you to do anything that you aren't ready for."

"It was hard. I'll admit that." Matthew sat back in his chair. "I think if I'd known Emily was out there when I found out, it would've been a little easier. If talking about our family tree would help someone else, then I guess I'm fine with it."

"I'll start making calls, writing my article and I'll tell Sam and Katie they can start making calls also." Abigail smiled. "I think this will be good for both of you."

****

Abigail caught a glimpse of John and Martha standing behind the counter talking. She could only imagine what their conversation consisted of. John took off his apron which meant he had free time in the kitchen. After several times of Martha or John pointing in the direction of their table, Abigail motioned for John to join them.

"Are you guys going to introduce me?" John asked as he approached their table.

"Of course. Emily, this is John, Martha's son. John, this is Emily Clayton." Matthew motioned toward Emily.

"It's nice to meet you, Emily." John smiled as he extended his hand for her to shake.

"You too, John." Emily smiled and shook his hand.

"Are you just visiting Puckerbrush?" John asked.

"Yes. I made a special visit to meet Matthew. It turns out Matthew and I are related." Emily explained.

"Really?" John took the empty seat next to Emily. "You mind if I ask how?"

"Not at all, if it's all right with Matthew." Emily glanced Matthew's direction.

"It's fine with me. John's like a brother to me."

"That's nice to know." Emily smiled and glanced in John's direction.

"Besides, I'm sure Martha would tell him everything anyway. It's hard to keep a secret in Puckerbrush. Right, Abigail?" Matthew patted Abigail on the leg.

"Boy, that's the truth." Abigail remembered how everyone in Puckerbrush knew about her and Matthew before they even did.

"It seems, Matthew and I have the same grandfather. We were connected on the DNA site we both joined."

"That would make you what? Cousins?" John's expression was one of surprise and showed he was trying to make sense of the information.

"That's right." Matthew smiled. "I would say it's a weird feeling to know that I have someone related I didn't know about, but I know exactly how it feels."

"It had to be a surprise for you." John turned to ask Emily.

"It was. Definitely a surprise." Emily explained.

"Did you tell your family when you found Matthew?" John asked.

Emily hesitated. "There's only my mother and she wouldn't understand what I was telling her. You see, she has Alzheimer's."

"I'm sorry to hear that."

Abigail watched John's expression turn somber.

"Thank you. She's the reason I started the search. We knew she was adopted and I wanted to find out the medical history of her biological family."

"And you found Matthew." John smiled.

"Yes, I did. I'm glad he agreed to meet with me." Emily nodded and smiled.

"What did your husband say about you finding new family?"

Abigail noticed John pick up a napkin and nervously twist it between his fingers as he waited for her reply.

"I'm not married." Emily held up her left hand showing her bare ring finger.

Abigail flashed a smile at John when she noticed the relief on his face and the eagerness of Emily to let John know she wasn't married.

"I haven't asked you what you do for a living, Emily." Matthew leaned back in his chair.

Abigail knew this move. He was trying to give John a break from having to ask questions.

"I'm in the medical research field," Emily replied. "I did my graduate study at the University of Texas in Houston. I took a job with a pharmaceutical company doing research so I could move back closer to home and take care of my mother."

"Wow. That's impressive." Matthew said. "What's your field of research?"

"Alzheimer's." Emily shifted uncomfortably in her chair. "It's an ugly disease that touches my family. I decided to make it my field of study when my mother was diagnosed. I watched her decline when I was in college and I don't want anyone and their family to have to go through what I have. Also, I live with the knowledge I have a real possibility of developing the disease myself since I could carry the gene." Emily paused for a moment then broke the awkward silence enveloping the table. "That's why I question myself every time I forget a name or when I misplace something."

"I'm sure that's difficult for you." Abigail could see the pain in Emily's eyes. "I pray you'll find a cure in our lifetime."

"Me too," Matthew replied.

"I'm so sorry. I didn't mean to put everyone in a sad place. I've learned to deal with it and I'm doing everything I can to find a cure." Emily sat up in her chair and changed the subject to try and lighten the mood. "What do you do for a living, John?"

"My mother and I own the Puckerbrush Café. I do the cooking and my mom does the baking. She has more patience with measuring exact amounts and following a recipe than I do. I like to experiment a little more."

"It sounds like you two make a good team then." Emily smiled.

"They really do. Martha's apple pie is amazing and everything John makes is delicious. I haven't had anything on the menu that I didn't love. This was my favorite place to eat when I first came to Puckerbrush." Abigail thought back on the first time she walked through the front doors of the café.

"What brought you to Puckerbrush, Abigail?" Emily asked.

"I came here as a favor for my friend Sam I was telling you about earlier, to write an article about the Puckerbrush Centennial Celebration. I fell in love with the town and the sheriff so I moved here." Abigail patted Matthew's arm.

"What magazine?" Emily asked.

"*Small-Town Living*," Abigail replied.

"I think I read that article. It was wonderful." Emily said. "I knew about Puckerbrush when I learned about Matthew because of that article."

"Thank you. I appreciate you saying that." Abigail smiled.

"You said you came here as a favor. Do you freelance?" Emily asked.

"I do some freelance for my friends. Otherwise, I am a mystery author." Abigail explained.

"Would I know anything you've written." Emily asked.

"This is where I have to interrupt." Martha walked toward the table. "Abigail's also known as Leeza McBride. She's only one of the top-selling mystery writers. I've read every one of her books. They're fantastic."

"I've read a few of them myself." Emily nodded. "I can't believe I'm sitting at the table with the best-selling author, Leeza McBride."

"There are a lot of surprises in store for you here in Puckerbrush." Abigail laughed. "Believe me. The fun's just beginning."

CHAPTER EIGHT

Abigail left the table to let Matthew and Emily talk. John had reluctantly excused himself to tend to something in the kitchen. Abigail knew she had given them a lot to think about. Her idea to publish an article in a magazine, if Sam could find one to take the story, and do as many interviews on television or radio as possible meant they would have to open their past to the world. For now, their family history was only shared with the people closest to them. If they agreed to Abigail's plan, it meant they would have to let anyone who read her article into their past, into their thoughts, leaving their family history bared to the world. Maybe it would give them some contacts to help find other people they were related to.

Martha surprised Abigail when she walked up behind her, putting her hand on her shoulder. "Are you all right? You look like you've got a lot on your mind."

"I don't know, Martha." Abigail took a seat at the counter. "I'm asking so much from them."

"Yes, you are, but you're trying to give them the answers that Emily wants. You're helping them try to locate other relatives. I'm not so sure about Matthew though." Martha took a seat next to her.

"That's what I'm worried about." Abigail put her chin in her hands. "He's done so well accepting what he learned about his past. I'm afraid if I bring it all up to the surface again, he's going to go backward."

"I understand completely. That's what worries me." Martha patted her on the back. "Maybe you should talk to him a little more before you do anything you can't take back."

"I will. I promise." Abigail turned and attempted to smile at Martha, tears running down her face. "I don't want to hurt him again. I don't know if he would forgive me again."

"I know you don't and so does he. Just go slow with your idea." Martha ran her hand up and down Abigail's back attempting to calm her. "You'll know if it's not right."

"Thanks, Martha. You always know the right thing to say." Abigail leaned her head on Martha's shoulder.

"Anything for a friend."

****

Emily cleared her throat as she walked up behind Abigail and Martha. "I'm going to leave now. I wanted to tell you how much I enjoyed meeting you two."

"It was so nice to meet you." Abigail stood from her seat, slipping her hands in her apron pocket. She wanted to give Emily a hug, but she wasn't quite sure how to interact with her yet. She was Matthew's family which meant she was Abigail's family. She was also a stranger who probably needed time to adjust to everything new happening around her.

"You're going to come back and visit again, right?" John asked as he came from the kitchen and stood behind the counter. His expression told everyone around him he wanted to see Emily again.

Abigail decided to try and help him out. "Yes. Make sure you come back soon. We can get to know each other better."

"You're welcome to come visit and stay for a while anytime." Matthew put his arm around Abigail's waist as he stood next to her. "It's going to take some time to get used to the idea that I have other family."

"I know what you mean. I'll make sure to come back. I'd like to get to know everyone better. You guys have been very accepting of the situation. It means a lot to me that you welcomed me so openly." Emily smiled.

"You'll find everyone in Puckerbrush is like that. You won't meet a stranger." Abigail glanced at Matthew and smiled. "Right?"

"She's right. We're all like one big family. Whether you want us to be or not. Just ask Abigail." Matthew laughed.

"Thank you." Emily turned her gaze toward John. "I'm looking forward to spending time with you again. All of you."

Abigail caught the exchange between John and Emily. She could see there was something there. She had to make sure Emily returned for another visit or two.

Emily waved as she walked out of the café doors. Abigail looked at Matthew. "You got her address and cell number, didn't you?"

"I didn't think about it. I have her email address. I can always email her and ask." Matthew explained.

"I'll go get it from her. You might need it, Abigail." John ran from behind the counter and out the café door to catch Emily before she drove away.

Martha, Abigail and Matthew moved to the window laughing as they watched John and Emily talking.

"I think the two of them hit it off." Martha smiled.

"I hope he remembers to get her information." Abigail laughed. "You know how guys are when a woman gets in their head."

"You women have this strange ability to turn men's minds into mush." Matthew kissed Abigail's forehead. "God help us."

****

"Did Emily say when she was coming back to Puckerbrush?" Martha smiled at Abigail as John walked back through the café door.

"Soon, I guess." John kept walking toward the kitchen with a smile on his face.

"Soon?" Martha exclaimed. "You mean you didn't ask here when you two were out there talking? As long as you were out there talking, I would think you would have a least asked her to come back for dinner or something."

"She'll be back this Friday night all right." John snapped an answer. "I told her I'd make her dinner."

"That's my boy!" Martha laughed. "He takes after his father. Offer to cook for a woman and she'll say yes every time."

"Are we welcome to come back and see her or is this dinner a date?" Matthew asked. "I just want to clarify before Martha and Abigail try to butt in on what you're planning to be a quiet dinner between you and Emily."

"Butt in!" Abigail exclaimed, hands on her hips. "Exactly what do you mean by that?"

"Come on ladies. You know you were planning to show up Friday night." Matthew laughed.

Martha glanced at Abigail and smiled. The two of them didn't say a word.

"See. I told you. You might as well make enough food for four, John." Matthew smiled. "You're probably going to have company.

"I'm only making enough food for two. You guys are on your own. I don't need you two tagging along to make sure I say and do the right thing. I think I can handle this on my own." John walked back into the kitchen not waiting for a reply from either Martha or Abigail.

"You heard the man." Matthew pointed toward the kitchen door. "You need to make other plans for Friday night."

"We weren't planning to sit at the same table with John and Emily." Martha explained.

"What were you planning then?" Matthew asked.

"Maybe sit at the table next to them." Martha's voice was quiet as she looked down at the floor.

"I was planning to have dinner with you, Matthew. Just because we're having dinner at the same time and at the same place doesn't mean I was going to butt in on their date." Abigail explained.

"Sure." Matthew nodded his head. "That makes perfect sense."

"Give us a little more credit would you." Martha smiled.

"I will when both of you give John space and let him have a nice, quiet date with Emily. If everything works out, John might end up being my cousin...or whatever or however he would be related."

Abigail and Martha laughed at Matthew's expression as he searched for the answer. "Let's just leave it at cousin."

"Wait. I forgot." Martha exclaimed as she turned and looked at Matthew. "I won't be able to butt in."

"Why not?" Abigail asked.

"I'm going to have to help out in the kitchen because John will be on his date." Martha snapped her fingers together. "Dang it."

"You're going to miss out then. I guess we're going to have to keep you filled in on how it goes." Abigail patted Martha's arm.

"We?" Matthew exclaimed. "I'm not doing anything of the sort. If you two want to stick your noses in the middle of John's date, that's up to you. I'm staying out of it."

"You better take really good notes. I want to know everything." Martha squeezed Abigail's hand. "I'm going to work." Martha turned and headed back toward the kitchen.

"It sounds like you're going to be busy Friday night." Matthew pulled Abigail close, wrapping his arms around her waist. "Wait until she finds out you haven't told her about the baby."

CHAPTER NINE

"I know you'll be happy with the ratings you receive from this interview, Cathy." Abigail tried to stay calm when she wanted to jump through the phone and hug the producer of the morning show. "We'll be at the station next Saturday bright and early. Thank you again for letting Matthew and Emily tell their stories."

Abigail ended her call, stood up from her office chair and jumped up and down a few times. "We're closer to finding the rest of the family. I've got to tell Matthew."

Picking up the piece of paper she had jotted down all the information on, Abigail headed out of the back door of the café and down the street to the sheriff's office. Matthew was sitting behind his desk making notes in a file.

"Are you busy?" Abigail leaned against the door frame waiting for Matthew's answer.

"You're a beautiful surprise." Matthew stood up and met Abigail halfway with a hug and kiss.

"I should come visit you more often if that's the greeting I receive." Abigail smiled.

"What are you doing here? I thought you were working on your book. You know Martha's gonna to be very upset if she finds out you're out running around and aren't behind your laptop writing." Matthew shook a finger at her.

"I know, but this is a very important visit." Abigail showed Matthew the piece of paper in her hand. "I just got a call from Cathy."

"Who's Cathy?" Matthew asked before she could explain.

"Cathy just happens to be the producer of the local CBS affiliate morning news show. She wants you and Emily to be on this Saturday's show." She handed him the piece of paper with the time and location of the studio, holding her breath as she waited for his reaction.

He studied the paper. "We'd have to leave Friday and spend the night in San Angelo so we could be at the studio that early Saturday morning."

"I thought about that. I was going to see what you thought before I called Emily. I even thought maybe we could call her together." Abigail waited for a reply.

"Let's call her now. We'll see what she says. If she agrees, I'll call and make reservations at a hotel close to the studio."

Abigail gusted out a sigh of relief.

Matthew walked back behind his desk and dialed his phone. He put the call on speaker so they both could hear what Emily said.

"Hello." Emily answered.

"Hi, Emily. It's Matthew and Abigail."

"Hi guys. It's good to hear from you. What's up?"

"Abigail just got off the phone with Cathy." Matthew glanced at Abigail to make sure he got the name right. "She's the producer of the CBS local affiliate's morning show. They want you and me to be on the show this Saturday. Are you up for it?"

"Wow. That's great. Yes, I'm up for it, if you are." Emily answered.

"It's an early show so we would have to drive down Friday and spend the night in San Angelo so we'd be there early Saturday morning. If you agree, I'll make reservations at a hotel close to the studio." Matthew waited for Emily's reply.

"I can do that. What if I come to Puckerbrush Friday afternoon and we can drive there together? I can say hello to John and Martha while I'm there."

Abigail smiled at Matthew as he shook his head. She remembered the exchange between Emily and John when she came to Puckerbrush the first time. Their Friday night date went well according to the texts Martha sent her. There was a lot of laughs, meaningful glances and even some hand touching which was a good sign. There was definitely something there and she approved.

"We're good with that. We'll see you Friday afternoon. Call if you have any questions before then." Matthew looked at Abigail to see if she had anything else to say.

"Wear something comfortable. We'll talk about everything on the way there, Emily. I can't wait to see you again." Abigail tried to think of anything else she needed to share with Emily.

"Thanks for calling guys. See you Friday."

"I'm going to have a famous fiancé after this weekend." Abigail wrapped her arms around Matthew's neck.

"Like the one I have?" Matthew kissed her.

****

Abigail watched from the side of the stage. The woman in charge of makeup was touching up the makeup of the hostess of the show, Michelle, before they went live. She had a perfect view and could see Emily was a little nervous because she was shifting in her chair. She and Matthew were chatting while they waited. Abigail hoped Matthew was sharing the suggestions she gave him to take deep breaths and try not to use your hands too much when you were talking. Other than that, she told him to not look at the cameras and forget they were even there. She took a quick minute to close her eyes and say a prayer. Hopefully Eldon was watching over them. She knew he had to be here with them today.

When Abigail opened her eyes, she saw a cameraman holding his hand up in the air and beginning the countdown to when they were live.

"Welcome to *AM San Angelo*. My guests today are Emily Clayton and Matthew Thompson. I've been looking forward to having them on my show because Emily and Matthew found out only a few months ago they are cousins." After a dramatic pause, Michelle continued. "This is a very interesting story and I'm going to let Emily tell it." Michelle pointed to Emily for her to begin.

Emily cleared her throat. "My mother, Dorothy, was adopted as a baby and a few years ago was diagnosed with Alzheimer's so I began searching for family members for medical research purposes. You see, my field of research is Alzheimer's because of my mother. As I found relatives I didn't know I had, Matthew was the only one who was interested in talking to me."

"Relatives? How many other people did you try to contact?" Michelle asked.

"Four other people." Emily paused.

"Four!" The tone of Michelle's voice rose a few octaves.

Abigail held her breath as she waited for Emily to answer.

"The others didn't return my emails so I have no way to find out who they are. I can't get names without their permission."

"And Matthew, you answered Emily's email why?" Michelle pointed to Matthew.

Abigail's heart began to beat faster. She knew how Matthew hated to talk about what he had learned about his family. She realized he was doing this for Emily and for himself to try and move past his anger and hurt. She knew he wanted to find the truth. "You can do this, Matthew." She whispered.

"I answered Emily's email because I was searching. I had learned shortly before Emily contacted me that my father was the illegitimate son of a traveling evangelist who held a revival in our town, Puckerbrush. The evangelist took advantage of my biological grandmother leaving her unmarried and pregnant with his child, my father."

"Did your grandmother, Mary, tell you this?" Michelle checked her notes.

This was hard for Matthew. Abigail could see it in his body language. She could also tell he was trying. What she wouldn't give to see one of those smile she loved on his face, but she knew that wasn't going to happen. Not right now.

"Yes. I mean no." Matthew paused. "Yes, her name was Mary and no, she didn't tell me. I never got the chance to meet my biological grandmother."

"Come on Matthew." Abigail whispered.

"Can you share a little of your story with us of how you found out about your father being adopted and the traveling evangelist being his father?" Michelle asked.

"Sorry. Yes." Matthew took a deep breath and continued. "My now fiancée, Abigail, came to Puckerbrush to write an article about Puckerbrush's Centennial Celebration and while she was there, she uncovered the story of the traveling evangelist as she researched her article. I not only learned my father was the evangelist's illegitimate son, but I also learned my biological great-grandfather was one of the people in Puckerbrush I had known all my life."

"You can do it." Abigail sighed. "I'm so proud of you, Matthew."

"Finding out all of that information must have turned your world around." Michelle asked.

"Yes, it did. Emily contacting me has helped me a lot." Matthew said.

"How is that?" Michelle waited for a reply.

"I was feeling pretty sorry for myself when I first found out. With the help of my fiancée and my family in Puckerbrush I was able to put everything in perspective. I couldn't change what happened to my biological grandmother."

"Mary, your biological grandmother, died in childbirth correct?" Michelle gazed at Matthew waiting for his answer.

"Yes, I learned that when I learned about my biological great-grandfather, Eldon. When Emily contacted me, I realized we had a connection. I suddenly wanted to learn everything I could about my family."

"I understand you brought a picture of the traveling evangelist that was taken and printed in the *Puckerbrush Newspaper* which is no longer in print. Let's show that picture." Michelle turned to look at a monitor. "I understand you don't know the name of the traveling evangelist and this is the only picture you know of, correct?" Michelle returned her gaze to Emily and Matthew.

"Yes, it's the only picture we know of and no, we don't know his name." Emily answered. "That's why we're here. We would like anyone who might recognize the man in this picture to call Matthew or me."

"We're going to put that information you gave us up on the screen for our audience. I hope there is someone out there who can help you find who this man is. I'm so happy the two of you agreed to share your story with us today. I wish you luck on your search." Michelle shook each of their hands then turned to the camera. "We'll leave the picture Matthew and Emily provided us up on the screen for a few more seconds. We'll be back after these messages."

"You guys did great." Abigail waited to greet Matthew and Emily as they exited the stage. "You answered all her questions without hesitating. I'm proud of both of you."

"Thank goodness Matthew was there because I was nervous. It helped having you next to me." Emily patted Matthew's arm.

"She asked some good questions," Matthew replied. "The picture you provided them from the old newspaper should help. I hope the right people watched and we find out if there really is anyone else out there we're related to."

"This is the first of it. The article I wrote is going to be published in a magazine of a friend of Sam's, *Ancestry Journal Magazine*, in the next week or two. Sam was going to call in a few favors but he didn't have to after other editors read my article. They published it willingly. Hopefully we'll get some more requests for interviews either on television or radio after people see you guys this morning." Abigail smiled.

"It's a little scary to think we put ourselves out there and shared personal information with so many people. If that's what it takes to get the answers we want, then it's worth it." Emily said.

"If it gets too much for you two, we can stop. You don't have to do this if it starts getting uncomfortable." Abigail watched the expression on both Matthew and Emily's faces. She remembered how learning about his past was hard for Matthew to deal with at first. The last thing she wanted was to take him back to that by having him share his life with the world.

"Let's take it one thing at a time." Matthew looked at Emily. "What do you say?"

"I think that's a great idea." Emily said. "If it gets too much, we stop."

"It's a deal." Matthew put his arm around Abigail as he agreed with Emily. "Let's get something to eat. I was too nervous to eat before the show but now I'm starving."

"Me too," Emily replied as she led the group out the front door of the studio.

****

"This is a nice café." Abigail looked around the restaurant. The Puckerbrush Café was a not quite as big but it was much homier. Maybe it was because this room was filled with a lot of strangers. When she ate at the Puckerbrush Café, she was surrounded by friends and family.

"What do you guys have planned for the rest of the weekend?" Emily asked.

Abigail looked at Matthew as she answered. "We're going to try and do some cleaning around the house. My parents and my Uncle Charles are coming into town in a week."

"That's right. Your wedding is in two weeks. I let you know I was planning to come, didn't I?" Emily asked.

"Yes, you did. You're coming with John, right?" Abigail waited for Emily's response.

"I am." Emily smiled.

"You two are enjoying getting to know each other, aren't you?" Abigail asked after she noticed Emily's expression at the mention of John's name.

"Be careful how you answer." Matthew laughed. "What every you say will go straight back to Martha."

"That's not true." Abigail slapped Matthew lightly on the arm.

"It's okay. I don't mind talking about it. I really like Martha and I know she and John are very close. I like the idea of that. I miss my mother. She's physically here but not mentally. John and I've been talking on the phone quite a bit lately and you're right, I'm enjoying getting to know John. I look forward to getting to know him better."

Abigail could see the change in Emily's expression. Remembering what she said about her mother having Alzheimer's made her wonder about their relationship. She couldn't imagine how hard it had to be to not have your mother to talk to or share with. Abigail remembered telling her mother when she had met someone new. When she'd gone on a first date, she would come home and tell her mother all about it. Not having that person to share with had to be hard.

"Martha and John are very close. Martha and I've become very close also. I don't think Martha meets anyone she doesn't like." Abigail tried to think of what to say to make the conversation easier for Emily. "I hope we get to talk to you after the wedding. I'm sure things will be a little crazy that day."

"Maybe at the reception." Emily said. "I'm sure we'll see each other there."

Abigail tried to think of other things the three of them could talk about. She got the feeling family was not a subject Emily was comfortable with. Before she could say anything, the waitress showed up with menus and glasses of water. Abigail decided for now to enjoy the quiet as they searched through their menus selecting what they each wanted to eat. They'd gotten up early to be at the studio and they were all tired. She attempted to quiet the writer in her who wanted to know everything about Emily's life for now and let Emily lead the conversation after they ordered.

CHAPTER TEN

"Mom, Dad." Abigail greeted her parents as they climbed out of their car in Matthew's driveway. "How was your drive?"

"It wasn't bad at all." Daniel Stratford hugged his daughter.

Abigail missed her father's hugs. She always felt safe when his strong arms wrapped around her. As he aged, he managed to stay in shape. It must have been something he learned during his army service. He had lost a little more of his hair though. Abigail knew better than to point it out.

"Hi, Mom." Abigail ran around the car to hug her mother but had to wait until she finished redoing her ponytail. Her hair was greying, and she still wore it shoulder length which Abigail approved of. She didn't want her to cut it short like most women her age did. Abigail loved the length and the salt and pepper look on her.

Matthew finally made it down the front stairs and joined them in the driveway to greet her parents. "Welcome Mr. and Mrs. Stratford." Matthew shook both their hands.

"Call us Daniel and Carol, Matthew." Daniel Stratford insisted. "After all you're marrying our daughter in a few days. We're all going to be family."

"All right. Daniel and Carol, it is." Matthew smiled. "I hope you had a nice trip in from Arizona. Can I help you with your luggage?"

"Let's let the guys get the luggage, Mom. I want to show you around the house and where Matthew and I are getting married." Abigail took her mother's hand and led her into the house.

"This is really nice, Abigail. I love the floor plan. It has a nice-sized living room and dining area off the kitchen." Carol Stratford glanced around the house.

"Yes, it is nice. I told you about how Matthew rebuilt it after the fire didn't I?" Abigail asked.

"Yes, you did. That had to have been so horrible for him." Carol said. "I mean losing your parents and your family home."

"I'm sure it was. We really don't talk about it very much. I let him bring it up if we do. I know it would be devastating for me if I lost you guys that way." Abigail gave her mother a quick hug.

"Let's not talk about it then. Tell me all about the wedding plans." Carol smiled at her daughter.

"Come let me show you the back where the ceremony's going to be. It's so beautiful." Abigail took her mother's hand and led her out the back door to the deck.

Carol Stratford didn't say a word for a few seconds as she took in all the scenery. "It's absolutely beautiful here. It's so green and it goes forever. I knew it would be beautiful when you described it to me, but I didn't imagine just how much. I can just imagine how amazing your wedding is going to be."

"I know. I thought the same thing the first time I saw it." Abigail agreed.

"I can see why you want to get married here." Carol smiled.

"It's a very special place for Matthew and I. I couldn't imagine getting married anywhere else." Abigail remember the first night she and Matthew spent together. This was where they shared their first kiss. This is where she realized she had fallen in love with him. This is where she found him when she came to tell him goodbye, thinking she had lost him forever. This is where he let her know he wanted her in his life. It was only right that this is where they become husband and wife.

"We put your luggage in the guest room." Matthew walked out on the deck.

"Thank you, Matthew." Carol turned and smile at him. "Your house is so beautiful. Abigail was showing me where you're going to have the wedding."

Matthew moved closer and put his arm around Abigail kissing her softly on the cheek. "This place is very special to us."

"That's just what I was telling Mom." Abigail smiled.

"You two look very happy." Carol said. "That makes me very happy."

"Thanks, Mom." Abigail smiled.

"This is such a big change for you, Abigail. I mean going from your small apartment in Chicago to this." Carol Stratford waved her arm through the air. "But I can see it suits you. I can see how happy all this and Matthew makes you."

"It does make me happy, Mom. I've never been happier." Abigail smiled as she looked at Matthew.

"I would have never imagined you settling down in a small town. I always pictured you living somewhere bigger and busier. I can see where this is a nice change though. It's so peaceful and quiet." Carol looked out in the distance.

"You're going to love everyone here in Puckerbrush. They're all like family." Abigail touched her mother's arm.

"I can't wait to meet them. The way you tell me about them when we talk makes me feel like I already know them." Carol smiled.

"After you and Dad get settled, we'll go to the café for dinner. You can meet Martha and John for a start."

"I can't wait. Let's go find your father and we'll get ready." Carol walked back through the back door. Abigail and Matthew followed.

****

"Welcome to Puckerbrush." Martha came from behind the counter and greeted Abigail, her parents, and Matthew as they walked through the door of the café. "You must be Mr. and Mrs. Stratford. I've heard so much about you two. I feel like I know both of you already."

"You must be Martha." Carol Stratford's tone was one of hesitation.

Abigail smiled, the look on her mother's face reminding her how she felt when she first met Martha. She'd never met anyone who had such an outgoing personality. It was as if Martha had known her all her life. She never met a stranger. Abigail knew for her and her mother, Martha's personality was one they'd never known before.

"It's good to see you, Martha." Abigail gave her a quick hug. "This is my father, Daniel." She pointed to her father who had a similar look on his face as her mother. "I wanted them to meet you and John first."

"How sweet of you." Martha smiled. "You have a beautiful, talented daughter. She's been a wonderful addition to Puckerbrush, plus I'm a huge fan of her writing."

"Abigail mentioned you had read all her books." Carol Stratford's expression finally turned to a more accepting one. "She is very talented."

"Why don't you guys find a table. I'll bring you menus and some water." Martha smiled.

Abigail picked her favorite table by the window and took a seat. "This is the table I always sat at when I was first here in Puckerbrush. You have a perfect view of whatever's going on outside."

"It's a very nice view, but does much go on here in Puckerbrush?" Daniel Stratford asked.

Matthew couldn't help but laugh. "I believe that's one of the first questions your daughter asked me.

"Like father like daughter," Abigail replied.

"What was your answer?" Daniel asked.

"I seem to remember telling her that after a hard day of working on the farm, most people have dinner with their families at home in Puckerbrush. Small towns are a different way of living than larger towns like Chicago."

"Plus, most of the women in Puckerbrush know how to cook." Abigail added. "I'm afraid I'm a little lacking in that area. Matthew's been teaching me what he knows."

"We've been learning together." Matthew reached across and took Abigail's hand.

"It's a good thing you have this nice café then." Carol Stratford laughed.

"I love having these two show up for lunch or dinner." Martha set glasses of water on the table in front of each of them and then handed out the menus. "It's like having dinner with family. Abigail and Matthew can fill you in on what are their favorites but the special tonight is chicken fried steak. It comes with mashed potatoes and gravy and corn."

"I think that sounds good." Daniel Stratford handed his menu back to Martha. "I don't even have to look at the menu."

"I agree." Matthew handed his menu back to Martha also.

"Make that three." Abigail did the same.

"I have to fit into the dress I brought for the wedding so I think I'll have the chef salad." Carol Stratford handed her menu back to Martha. "Ranch dressing on the side, please."

"You got it. Don't forget to tell them about the apple pie." Martha winked at Abigail as she turned to walk away.

"Apple pie?" Daniel Stratford asked.

"Oh, you haven't lived until you've had a piece of Martha's delicious apple pie." Matthew smiled.

"It's really good. You have to try some." Abigail agreed.

"Welcome to the Puckerbrush Café."

Abigail turned to see who Martha was greeting. "Uncle Charles!" Abigail stood up from the table and ran toward her uncle. "It's so good to see you. Why didn't you call and let me know you were here?" Abigail asked as she gave her uncle a hug, sinking into his arms like she did her father's. Charles was a little squishier than her father, but they looked so much alike. The same height and similar facial expressions. They were two of her favorite men.

"I was talking to Berta." Charles rolled his eyes. "She told me I would probably find you here. I decided I would surprise you."

"If what you mean to say is that if you would have stopped to call me, you would have never gotten away from Berta?" Abigail whispered.

"Exactly." Charles agreed.

"Come sit down at the table with us. We're just ordering dinner." Abigail took Charles' hand and led him to the table where Carol, Daniel, and Matthew were already standing ready to greet him.

"Hello everyone." Charles gave Carol a hug and shook Daniel's hand. "You must be Matthew."

"I am." Matthew shook his hand. "It's nice to meet you, Mr. Stratford."

"Charles, please. Mr. Stratford was my father." Charles laughed.

"All Abigail's been able to talk about is how you were coming to Puckerbrush to perform our wedding ceremony. She's been looking forward to it." Matthew smiled.

"I'm glad. She promised me when she was a little girl that I'd be the one to marry her." Charles laughed. "I'm glad she remembered."

"How could I forget?" Abigail smiled. "You're my favorite uncle."

"I'm you're only uncle. On your father's side that is." Charles said. "I have to be your favorite."

"There's that." Abigail agreed.

"It's great of you to come all this way to perform the wedding ceremony, Charles." Daniel said. "We all appreciate it."

"It's my pleasure. Besides, you don't think I would let my favorite niece get married before I met the man she was going to marry." Charles looked at Matthew.

"Do you want me to add another special to your order for this handsome gentleman?" Martha asked as she handed Charles Stratford a menu and placed a glass of water on the table in front of him.

"Martha, this is my uncle, Charles Stratford. He came to Puckerbrush to from Chicago to perform our wedding ceremony." Abigail introduced the two as Charles stood from his chair, took Martha's hand and placed a kiss gently on the back.

"It's a pleasure to meet you, Charles" Martha blushed like a school girl.

"It's my pleasure, Martha." Charles smiled as he held on the Martha's hand a little longer.

Abigail watched the exchange between the two. She'd never seen Martha act this way. She normally treated everyone with the same outgoing personality Abigail had come to know. Something about Uncle Charles made Martha soften just a little around the edges.

"Three of us are having the special which is chicken fried steak, mashed potatoes and gravy with corn. Do you want to join us?" Abigail asked.

"The special sounds wonderful to me." Charles looked into Martha's eyes as he finally let go of her hand.

"Four specials and a chef salad with dressing on the side coming right up." Martha continued meeting Charles' gaze. "Don't forget about the apple pie."

Abigail glanced at Matthew as Martha finally turned to walk back toward the kitchen. This time in slow motion as if Charles had placed a spell on her. "What's with that?" she mouthed to Matthew.

Matthew shrugged his shoulders as he turned to watch Martha make her way through the kitchen door. "You certainly have a way with women, Charles."

CHAPTER ELEVEN

"Are you sure there's nothing I can do to help?" Abigail asked as she watched Martha working behind the counter.

Leaving her mother and father at the house to relax and recover from their trip to Puckerbrush, Abigail woke with Matthew, and left for the café. She felt like she was putting a lot on Martha's plate, preparing for the rehearsal dinner and wedding reception, and if she could help in anyway, she would feel a lot better about it.

"I can't think of anything. John and I have everything under control. I've managed to keep his focus on you and Matthew and off Emily. I can't say it's been easy. Those two are really getting close." Martha rolled her eyes.

"Are you good with that?" Abigail asked.

"I am. John is happy, so I'm happy. Anyway, we're going to bring everything out to the house tomorrow night for the rehearsal dinner. Then we'll have hors d'oeuvres, cake and punch here at the café after the wedding." Martha smiled. "And Berta has all the decoration under control."

Abigail watched as Martha seemed lost in her thoughts.

"And before I forget, I talked to Berta about turning the old *Puckerbrush Newspaper* building into a museum and she's on board and wants to meet with us to talk about it. I told her it would have to wait until after the wedding because we were busy until then." Martha returned to cleaning the same spot on the counter.

"I'd forgotten we were going to call Berta. That was the day Emily came to town and we got interrupted. I'm glad you remembered." Abigail had known Martha long enough to know when there was something on her mind. Today there was something either bothering her or something she was trying to find the right time to bring it up.

"What's on your mind, Martha." Abigail decided she would just ask instead of waiting until the time was right for Martha to blurt it out.

"I don't know what you mean." Martha continued cleaning the same spot on the counter she had been cleaning for the past ten minutes.

"You said you managed to keep John's focus on the wedding. What about you? You have something on your mind. Why don't you just tell me what it is so you don't rub a hole in the counter top cleaning that same spot." Abigail pointed to the towel in Martha's hand that was making circles over and over.

Tossing the wet towel into the tub underneath the counter, Martha smiled. "There's something I wanted to ask you."

"I knew it. What is it?" Abigail placed her elbows on the counter and leaned in.

Martha moved closer to the end of the counter where Abigail was sitting. "I don't want to seem nosy, but why's your Uncle Charles single?" Martha blushed as she looked down at her feet.

"Martha, I don't think I've ever seen you blush." Abigail chuckled. "It's cute." Abigail wondered if Martha and her Uncle Charles had hit it off. Charles did stay at the café after they left. He said he wanted to finish his apple pie, but Abigail knew better.

Martha covered her cheeks with her hands. "I'm not blushing. It's warm in here."

"Sure." Abigail laughed.

"I didn't want to ask Charles. I mean, we just met last night and we didn't have much time to talk. I don't think it's right to ask such a personal question so soon. Do you?" Babbling away, Martha leaned against the counter.

"It wouldn't stop me, but I can see your point." Abigail straightened up and placed her hands in her lap. "Where do I begin?"

Martha waited, an expectant look on her face.

"Uncle Charles has been divorced for I believe twenty years." Abigail looked up as she tried to calculate how many years it had been. "I was around five or six so that would be about right." Abigail nodded. "He married a woman he met in college. He was so in love with her. They had three daughters. Then, one day she left him."

"Why?" Martha asked as she waited for Abigail to continue. "You can't leave me with just that much."

"Uncle Charles doesn't talk about her much so getting the story from him would be next to impossible. According to my father though, Uncle Charles didn't provide the lifestyle Aunt Guinevere was accustomed to, so she took their daughters and moved back home to live with her parents who could give her that lifestyle."

"You have to be joking!" Martha exclaimed. "If she didn't love him, why did she marry him?"

Abigail shrugged. "From what my father said, they were very much in love. Uncle Charles was crazy about her and she about him. The problem was they came from different backgrounds. Aunt Guinevere was brought up with maids and servants. Her father's family was extremely wealthy. She never lifted a finger around the house. All she had to do was look pretty which she did very well." Abigail smiled as she pretended to straighten her hair.

"Uncle Charles felt they should live within their means, and they didn't need such an extravagant lifestyle. That made Aunt Guinevere unhappy. Her parents wanted her to be happy and were always trying to give her money so she could hire help. Uncle Charles refused to accept it. He's a very proud man who wanted to provide for his family himself."

"I can see that." Martha interrupted.

"Me too, but Aunt Guinevere couldn't. She didn't know how to do anything when they were first married. She couldn't cook. She'd never done laundry. She'd never cleaned. It was all new to her and I guess she was horrible at it. Uncle Charles took on a lot of that responsibility. When he would come home from work, she would still be in her pajamas." Abigail took a sip of her tea.

"He said she made a lot of trips to visit her parents especially after their daughters were born. I guess one of the times she said she was going to visit her parents, she took the girls and never came back."

"Oh, that's so sad." Martha sighed. "Charles had to have been heartbroken."

"He still is. I think that's why he's never found anyone new. I think he's been waiting for her to come back to him." Abigail leaned against the counter and fixed her gaze on Martha. "Maybe it's going to take someone like you to help him forget her."

"Taking the place of a first love is a hard thing to do." Martha frowned. "It's been hard for me to even think of replacing John's father."

"How many years has he been gone?" Abigail asked.

"Twenty-five years now." Martha placed her hand on her heart. "Sometimes it's like he was just here yesterday. Every time I look at John, I see his face."

"I'm sure he would want you to be happy. I don't think he would want you to be alone just because you still love him. No one is ever going to take his place. You just have to make room for someone new." Abigail reached across the counter for Martha's hand.

"I know." Martha took Abigail's hand and smiled. "I've told myself that for a long time. No one has ever made me even consider it until now."

"You mean until you met my Uncle Charles." Abigail smiled.

"Until I met your Uncle Charles." Martha agreed. "There's something about him that makes me want to... maybe give love another try."

"That's wonderful." Abigail squeezed Martha's hand. "Nothing would make me happier. Uncle Charles deserves a woman like you and you deserve someone like my Uncle Charles."

"He's coming here to have dinner. We aren't getting married or anything." Martha laughed and shook her head.

"You never know. Like I told you before, I saw the look you two gave each other and he did stay behind last night. Matthew already has Emily and John married off. I can do the same with you and Uncle Charles." Abigail laughed.

"He's just coming to have dinner." Martha insisted.

"We'll see. I bet that's what John says about Emily. She's just coming for dinner. We all know there's more there than dinner." Abigail smiled as she took another sip of her tea. There would be nothing that would make her happier than to see two people she loved find each other. Puckerbrush had that effect on people.

CHAPTER TWELVE

The day was even more beautiful than Abigail could have imagined. The sun was shining. The temperature was perfect and there was a light breeze to keep everyone comfortable. Stepping out on the deck, memories of how far she and Matthew had come flooded her mind. They'd gone from strangers to lovers and then she almost lost him. Now they were starting a life together full of possibilities. Her future was not what she'd thought it would be, it was so much better.

The deck railing was covered in sheer fabric intertwined with white daisies. There were rows of white wooden chairs separated by an aisle. At the end of the aisle was an altar overflowing with a mixture of white roses, daisies, and greenery which would be where Abigail would meet Matthew to pledge their love for each other.

A single row of six chairs was placed off to the side under a small tree. In each chair a white rose was placed in front of a framed photo.

In the first chair was Sister Angelica. Abigail had managed to find a photo in some of Eldon's belongings.

The second chair had a photo of Eldon. The photo was one Abigail had taken without him knowing. To her it caught the essence of who Eldon was, the Eldon she knew and loved.

In the third chair was an old, blurred black and white photo she had found in one of Eldon's journals. It was of Mary, Eldon's daughter, and Matthew's biological grandmother.

In the fourth chair was a photo of Abigail's grandmother. How she would have loved Matthew just as her parents had learned to in the short time they'd had to get to know him.

In the fifth and sixth chairs were photos of Matthew's mother and father.

Berta had done a beautiful job decorating. Her idea for chairs for all the people who were loved and had been instrumental in bringing Matthew and Abigail together, but couldn't be here to share this day with them except in spirit was a beautiful idea.

Abigail knew each of them were happy she and Matthew had found each other. She could feel the love coming from each of them.

"Don't you think you should come in and start getting dressed?" Martha, already dressed in a knee-length blue dress cinched at her small waist with a large belt and a pair of matching pumps, walked up behind her and put her hand on her shoulder.

"I will." Abigail placed her hand on top of Martha's. "You look beautiful."

"Thank you, but this is your day. We need to get you dressed."

"I was just thinking about my life and how happy I am. About how fate brought Matthew and I together."

"I'm so glad." Martha smiled. "You and Matthew are perfect for each other and you have a beautiful future ahead of you. Hopefully with a few children thrown in for good measure."

"Maybe someday." Abigail knew it wasn't the right time to tell Martha or anyone. She could almost see a little Matthew running through the yard with a dog following on his heels. She could hear the laughter and joy coming from him.

"Promise me you'll give it some thought. I'd love to have a few little ones running around again. Lord knows, John may not ever give me any grandchildren so I'll have to count on you and Matthew for that." Martha laughed.

"I promise I'll give it some thought but I wouldn't rule John out yet." Abigail turned and looked at Martha. "You'll make a wonderful, loving grandmother or aunt. Whichever you want to be."

Martha's voice started to shake as she hugged her. "Let's go get you dressed."

****

Matthew was waiting for Abigail in front of the altar. He looked so handsome in his dress blues. She fell in love with him all over again.

"You know your mother and I are very proud of you and whatever you do with your life is all right with us as long as you're happy. Your happiness is all that's important. I can tell Matthew makes you very happy but I do have to ask though, are you sure about this?" Daniel Stratford asked as he took Abigail's arm to walk her down the aisle.

Abigail turned and smiled. "I've never been so sure of anything in my life. Matthew does make me happy. Whatever my life brings after this, I know I want him to share it with me."

Daniel patted her arm. "Then let's get you married."

All she could see when they reached the end of the aisle was the smile she loved on Matthew's face. She took his hand and joined him in front of her Uncle Charles.

"You look beautiful." Matthew whispered.

"And you look very handsome." Abigail smiled.

The words her Uncle Charles said were only half registering. She could hear him speaking, but the feeling of love and happiness enveloped her.

Never knowing such love for another person existed, she'd never been so sure of anything in her life. She and Matthew belonged together and they were meant to share together everything that happened from today forward.

****

"Here's to the happy couple." Daniel Stratford put his arm around his wife's waist and raised his glass for the crowd to toast Abigail and Matthew.

Matthew leaned over and kissed Abigail lightly on the lips. Abigail squeezed his hand which she hadn't been able to let go of since they sat down at the head table.

She knew she had so many people to thank for today. This was the perfect time to do it. Abigail glanced around the room as she stood.

"I need to say thank you to my mother and father for coming to Puckerbrush to join us today. And my Uncle Charles for insisting he was the one who had to perform the ceremony. I love you guys." Abigail smiled and blew a kiss to her family.

"I want to thank Martha and John for the wonderful job they've done decorating the café for the wedding reception and for the delicious food all of you are about the eat. I also need to thank Berta for making my wedding so beautiful and the floral arrangements on each of the tables. Everyone in Puckerbrush has come together to make this day so special for Matthew and me. Thank you doesn't seem adequate. We love you all."

Abigail sat back down in her chair. She knew there was no possible way she could repay them for all the time and love they'd given. She also knew if she continued to thank them, she would end up in tears.

"That was perfect." Matthew took her hand under the table. "Mrs. Thompson."

That was the first time Abigail had heard those words. "Wow. That's me. Mrs. Abigail Thompson."

"Yes, it is." Matthew laughed.

"I hadn't thought about that." Abigail tilted her head sideways.

"If you want, I can change my name instead. Mr. Matthew Stratford sounds kinda regal." Matthew laughed. "Or Mr. Leeza McBride."

Abigail scrunched up her nose. "I don't know about that. You'll always be Matthew Thompson. The person I fell in love with."

"And you'll always be Abigail Stratford to me." Matthew leaned in and gave Abigail a kiss.

"What if I'm now Abigail Stratford-Thompson?" Abigail smiled. "I like that."

"That's settled then." Matthew laughed. "I'm glad we had this talk."

"Me too." Abigail smiled.

"Now why don't we have our first dance, Mrs. Stratford-Thompson? I think they're playing our song." Matthew stood from his chair and offered Abigail his hand.

"I'd love too." Abigail took his hand and they made their way to the dance floor. After a few moments and a lot of picture- taking, everyone else in the room joined the couple on the dance floor.

Abigail laid her head on Matthew's shoulder. This was a day she was never going to forget.

****

"Matthew. Abigail. There's someone I would like you to meet, Abigail." Piper joined them as they chatted with the other people in the room. "This is my father, Robert Piper." Piper put his hand on his father's shoulder. "You remember Matthew don't you Dad? I'm going to be covering for him the next two weeks while he's on his honeymoon."

"Of course. I remember Matthew. He came to our house many times with you for dinner after you guys met at the academy." Robert Piper offered his hand for Matthew to shake. "How could I forget?"

"Abigail has become a good friend also. We've gotten to know each other over the past few months." Piper smiled at Abigail.

"Abigail." Robert Piper offered his hand to Abigail also. "It's nice to meet you. Any friend of my son's is a friend of mine."

"It's a pleasure to meet you, Mr. Piper." Abigail could see the resemblance not only in features but also in height between father and son. Robert Piper was a handsome man. His head full of dark hair with touches of grey on the sides gave him a distinguished look.

"It's nice to see you again, Mr. Piper." Matthew said.

"You too, Matthew. Samuel will do a good job for you while you are on your honeymoon. I'm sure of it." Robert Piper laughed. "Samuel's a hard-working sheriff who keeps our small town safe. I'm very proud of him."

"Thanks, Dad." Piper patted his father on the back. "I'm the person I am because of you and all you taught me growing up."

"He's right." Abigail spoke up. "Both Piper and Matthew have been raised right. Both of them have manners and are very thoughtful and caring people. That's a rare quality in most young men these days. You should be proud of the job you and Mrs. Piper did with Samuel."

"Thank you, Abigail. I have to give most of the credit to my wife. She was the one who kept Samuel in line. When she passed a few years ago, it was a hard thing for both Samuel and I but enough of that talk." Robert Piper waved his hand in the air. "This is a day of joy. Thank you for allowing me to be part of your big day. I've enjoyed meeting your family and seeing how you and Matthew are part of the town. Puckerbrush is a good place to live and raise a family." Robert Piper smiled.

"We're glad you could join us." Matthew said.

"There's someone else I would like you to meet, Dad." Piper caught Emily's gaze, pulling her away from the group of people she was chatting with when he motioned for her to join them.

"This is Emily Clayton." Piper gave her a warm hug as she joined the group. "Emily, I'd like you to meet my father, Robert Piper.

"Emily." Robert extended his hand for her to shake.

"Emily and I just met at Matthew and Abigail's engagement party." Piper explained. "She's quickly become a friend."

Abigail watched the exchange between Piper and Emily hoping it was just a friendly one.

"It's nice to meet you." Emily shook Robert's hand and then turned her attention to Matthew and Abigail. "It was a beautiful ceremony. It was great to spend the afternoon with Piper, John, and everyone. Thank you so much for inviting me."

"Of course. You're family now." Matthew smiled. "It also gives me a chance to ask you if you received your letter to cease and desist."

"I did." Emily said. "I didn't want to bring it up at your wedding or reception. This is a day for celebration."

"I was going to call you last night, but we've been so busy with the wedding." Matthew said. "I thought we could talk about it when we get back from our honeymoon."

"I've cancelled the two interviews we had lined up with newspapers." Abigail interrupted. "They were very understanding about the reason why."

"What are you guys talking about?" Piper waved his finger between the three of them waiting for an answer to his question.

"It seems our grandfather has family out there who object to Emily and me showing the images of him Abigail found in the *Puckerbrush Newspaper* publicly, and searching for any more children he might have fathered." Matthew's expression let the group know how he felt about the situation.

"You mean the traveling evangelist has a family somewhere? Children? A wife? What?" Piper asked.

"We aren't sure." Matthew explained. "All we know is that Emily and I received a letter from a law firm informing us we would be sued by the family of the man in the photo if we continued to do TV interviews or write any more articles using the image we have and searching for additional children. It seems they believe we're lying."

"That's crazy. Did they tell you the family name or where the evangelist was from?" Piper asked.

"No. Nothing. They wanted to remain anonymous. Emily and I can only prove the two of us are related. We don't have DNA to prove the evangelist was our grandfather." Matthew explained.

Abigail listened to the conversation but was drawn to the expression on Robert Piper's face. It was one of surprise. She couldn't help but wonder what he was thinking.

"Dad, you remember me telling you about Matthew finding a long-lost cousin?" Piper asked his father. "That's Emily. Their grandfather was a traveling evangelist who brought his revival through Puckerbrush in the sixties."

Robert Piper didn't say a word. Abigail noticed his gaze lock on Emily and the coloring in his face disappear.

"Are you all right, Mr. Piper?" Abigail pulled out a chair from the closest table. "Here. Why don't you sit down. You look a little pale."

Abigail helped Piper make sure his father took a seat.

"What's wrong, Dad?" Piper knelt down next to his father. "You don't look so good."

"I don't know." Robert Piper finally answered. "I just got a little lightheaded. I'm fine now."

"Let me get you some water." Piper stood and took a full glass of water from the empty table next to them and handed it to his father. "Drink some of this. It'll help. Maybe we need to get you home so you can rest."

Robert Piper took a sip of the water and handed the glass back to his son. "Maybe I should go home. I hate to take you away from your friends."

"It's fine, Dad. I was planning to leave soon. Now that you've seen Matthew and met Abigail and Emily, we can go home." Piper placed his hand on his father's shoulder.

"Let me help you get him to the car." Matthew moved on the other side of Robert Piper.

Piper gave Abigail a quick hug and kiss on the cheek. "I'll see you when you guys get back from your honeymoon."

"Thank you for being part of our day. Take care of your father." Abigail attempted a smile as wonder filled her thoughts.

"It was great to see you again, Emily. Maybe we can all get together again soon." Piper gave her a hug and then took his father's arm to help him stand.

Abigail watched as Matthew and Piper helped Robert Piper to the car. There was something there. She had that feeling she got when something wasn't as it seemed. When she and Matthew returned from their honeymoon, finding out what was wrong would be her first project.

CHAPTER THIRTEEN

Emily

Opening her eyes to the small stream of morning sun shining through the blinds, Emily smiled as she curled up against the warmth of John's naked body lying next to her in bed. As he began to stir, she ran her hand down his chest. "Good morning."

With a delicious moaning sound, John reached for her, pulling her close. Kissing her forehead and working down to her mouth, he whispered, "Good morning."

"I'm starving." Emily laughed. "Can we call room service?"

John sat up on his elbow as he glanced down at Emily. "Maybe we can work out a deal."

"I like the way you're thinking." Emily wrapped her arms around John's neck, slowly pulling him closer. "Show me what you mean."

Without hesitation, John took his time showing Emily exactly what he meant.

****

Emily made herself at home by climbing up on the kitchen countertop as she watched a bare-chested John scramble eggs. She had taken his shirt when they climbed out of bed in the back room of the café which was definitely to her benefit. His moves were gentle and precise as he moved the eggs around the pan with a spatula as they cooked. She loved watching his hands work without even thinking about what he was doing. It reminded her of when they made love. He knew exactly what she wanted and how to please her. It was comfortable being with John. Something she had never known before. She felt as if they were two puzzle pieces who finally found where they belonged. She also realized it was time to talk.

"Those look so good." Emily smiled.

"Just wait until you taste them." John leaned over and kissed her.

"I feel so special having the entire café to just the two of us." Emily jumped down off the countertop as she watched John plate the eggs and take two pieces of toast out of the toaster, placing one on each plate.

"I'm glad you decided to stay after the wedding yesterday." John smiled.

"Me too." She knew she was taking a chance. Her feelings for John were growing. She had never met anyone who had the same effect on her as John.

"We have a few hours before the Sunday crowd starts showing up. Let's go sit down." John handed Emily one of the plates and motioned for her to follow him out the kitchen doors. "Sit down here at the counter. I'll get us a glass of milk and some coffee."

"I love, love, love being waited on. Did I ever tell you that?" Emily asked as she took a seat at the counter, picking up the piece of toast and taking a bite while she waited for John to get their milk, coffee, and forks.

"Here you go." John placed a fork beside her plate, a glass of milk in front of her and then poured her a cup of coffee. He stood behind the counter in front of her as he ate his eggs.

"Can we talk?" Emily asked as she took a bite of eggs.

"I guess so, if we have to." John laughed. "I thought you were hungry."

"I'm serious." Emily exclaimed. "I can talk and eat at the same time."

John reached across and took her hand. "I'm sorry. I was joking. Of course, we can talk. It sounds serious though."

"I guess it is serious." Emily put her fork down on her plate, leaned back and put her hands in her lap. "I'm really enjoying spending time with you. Everything has been moving a little fast with us. We've only known each other a little over a month." Emily paused. "I've never let anyone in before like I have you."

John walked from behind the counter and took a seat next to Emily at the counter. "I'm glad it's me you let in."

"Me too." Emily smiled as she took John's hand. "There's something I want to tell you before whatever it is between us goes any further."

"You can tell me whatever you want. I'm right here and I'm not going anywhere." John smiled.

"Knowing that makes this a little harder, but here goes." Emily took a deep breath. "When we first met, I told you about my mother having Alzheimer's."

"I remember."

"Well, what I didn't tell you is that I haven't been tested to see if I have the gene."

"Okay," John replied.

"I'm afraid to know and also if I do have the gene, it won't tell me for sure if I'm going to develop the disease. I want to take each day at a time, learn everything I can about the disease and hopefully help find a cure so if I find out I have the gene, there'll be a cure or at least something to help the symptoms and I won't have to suffer like my mother."

"I can understand that." John said. "I would probably feel the same."

"I also don't want anyone else, especially anyone I'm married to or in a relationship with to have to suffer like my mother and I have."

Emily took a breath before she continued. All the feelings and memories of the day she came home from college to find her father waiting for her to arrive with his bags packed sitting on the floor in front of him. She could remember what he said word for word as he attempted to make her understand why he couldn't stay. All she knew was for the first time since her mother was diagnosed, she was glad her mother was lost to both of them. She wouldn't have to deal with the hurt and disappointment of the person you love walking out on you.

"You see my father walked out leaving me to take care of Mom when she began forgetting who he was. He told me he didn't recognize her as the woman he married. The woman he married was gone." Emily paused again trying to keep her composure.

"He just walked out? How could he do that?" John interrupted the silence.

"I can't say I blame him." Emily shifted in her seat. "I know how hard it can be to realize your own mother doesn't know you. Or to realize your mother has forgotten everything about your childhood and how much she loved you and you loved her. I can't imagine if it was the person I was married to." Emily had to stop as she felt the tears puddling in her eyes.

"Why are you telling me this, Emily?" John asked, leaning forward, his long legs pressed against hers.

"I really like you, John. Like I said before, I've never let anyone in this close. I'm not sure how to handle it." Emily wiped a stray tear from her cheek.

"I can understand why you're afraid to let anyone in so we handle it like you handle the possibility you have the Alzheimer's gene. We take it one day at a time." John smiled.

Emily bowed her head as she tried not to break down. "Can I ask a huge favor then?"

"Yes." John reached over, put his fingers under her chin lifting her head so he could see her face. "Anything."

"Will you go with me to meet my mother?" Emily waited for his reply.

He didn't hesitate. "Of course. I'd love to meet your mother."

"I don't want you to think of this as a social visit. I want you to see what could be my future. I want you to have all the information you need to make a decision."

"A decision? What decision do you want me to make?" John asked.

"I'm giving you the opportunity to end our relationship now before it goes any further, if that's what you want. I don't want you to stick around and things become serious between us and then have you regret your decision. I want you to see how difficult it will be living with someone and loving someone who doesn't remember you or your life together." Emily watched the expression in John's eyes to see if she could tell what he was thinking.

"When do we leave?" John asked as he took both Emily's hands in his.

"I plan to go see Mom next Saturday. Do you think you could get away for a few hours? We could go whatever time's good for you." Emily waited for John's reply.

"I can get away for a few hours Saturday midmorning." John nodded, "Will that work?"

"Of course."

"Saturday it is." John kissed one of Emily's hands then pointed to her plate on the counter. "Now finish your breakfast."

****

"Are you sure you want to do this?" Emily placed her hand on John's arm before he opened the door.

"Sure. Why wouldn't I? This is important to you, so it's important to me." John smiled as he pulled the door open with his free hand and motioned for Emily to go ahead of him with the bouquet of flowers he was holding in his other hand.

"Her room's just down this hallway." Emily took his free hand as she led the way.

"Hi, Emily." A familiar voice came from behind. Emily turned around to see Susie walking behind them, her blonde hair pulled back in her normal ponytail, wearing blue scrubs which were hugging her larger body.

Emily and John stopped and waited for her to catch up.

"If you're here for a visit, I should tell you your mother's having another bad day today."

"I guess I should've called before we drove out." Emily turned and glanced at John. "John, this is Susie. She's one of my mother's nurses. Susie, this is John. He's a friend of mine."

"It's nice to meet you, John." Susie held her hand out for John to shake. "How do you two know each other? Do you work together?"

Emily wasn't sure she approved of Susie's curiosity.

"No." John looked in Emily's direction as he waited for her to finish answering Susie's question.

"John lives in Puckerbrush. We met through mutual friends." Emily explained. "We're going to stop in and say hello to Mother. I wanted John to meet her."

"You know how Dorothy can be when she's having a bad day. Do you think it's a good idea? Maybe you and John can come back on a day she's doing a little better." Susie glanced at the bouquet of flowers in John's hand. "I don't think those will even cheer her up."

From the expression on Susie's face, Emily knew she was trying to tell her without coming out and saying it directly that her mother was being difficult. Emily knew just how difficult she could be on days like today. She didn't envy Susie the job of taking care of her mother.

"We don't plan to stay long." Emily smiled. "I just want to see her since we're already here."

This was a perfect day for John to meet her mother. Days like today were the reason her father walked out. He didn't know how to take care of her and he wasn't willing to learn. The point she tried to get across to John was this could be their future if they continued in the relationship that John so desperately wanted. Her chances of ending up exactly where her mother was were very high.

The idea of being in a long-term relationship was something she'd not contemplated. At least not until she'd met John. He was the first man for whom she'd second-guessed her decision. She needed him to understand what he was asking of her by not letting her go.

Emily had done everything she could think of to keep John at bay. She stopped returning his calls and emails for a few days. She avoided him the time he delivered her flowers at work. He was very persistent and she was finding it more difficult to keep from falling for him.

Spending the night with him after the wedding was something she hadn't planned, but after a few glasses of champagne and slow dances, it wasn't difficult for John to convince her. She already found him attractive.

If John meeting her mother on one of her most difficult days didn't convince him what could be ahead, Emily was at a loss for ideas. When or if she ended up in the same condition as her mother, she wouldn't know. It would be up to John to decide how to take care of her. Would he be the kind of man who would stay or would he be like her father and walk out? She really wanted him to know what he was getting himself into if they let their relationship become serious.

She took John's free hand and continued down the hallway to her mother's room. Dorothy was sitting in her chair by the window. The curtains were drawn and the room was dark. Emily let go of John's hand and motioned for him to stay there while she moved closer to her mother. "Hi, Mother. It's me Emily."

Dorothy didn't move. She kept looking straight ahead not even reacting to the sound of Emily's voice. Reaching over and pulling one of the curtains back to let in a little outside light, Emily stopped when she heard a groaning sound coming from her mother.

"It's very dark in here. I thought you might want a little light? It's a beautiful day outside." Emily tried to keep the tone in her voice upbeat but the groaning continued just not as strong.

"There's someone I would like you to meet, Mother." Emily walked over and took John's hand not waiting for any response from her mother. She led him closer to the chair. "This is John. He's a friend of mine." Emily watched for any response, but there was nothing. She turned and looked at John hoping she could see how this was affecting him.

"It's nice to meet you, Mrs. Clayton." John reached down and lightly touched Dorothy's hand which she quickly pulled back. John didn't let that stop him. "Emily invited me to come with her to meet you and I was happy to. I thought you might like some flowers to brighten your room."

Dorothy turned and looked at John and smiled. "I'm happy you came." For a moment, the fog lifted, and Emily saw the joyful woman who had raised her.

Emily's expression must have told John how surprised she was as he reached and took her mother's hand. "Emily talks about you a lot so I was happy to come with her today." John sat down on the edge of a table that was next to Dorothy's chair as she returned to staring straight ahead.

Emily reached to take the flowers from John's hand when her mother put out a hand and stopped her. "John brought those for me."

"I was going to lay them on you bed tray until we could see if Susie could find a vase to put them in. They'll look pretty by your bed."

"I'll keep them." Dorothy pulled the bouquet of flowers close to her chest. "They smell wonderful, John. Thank you."

"I'm glad you like them. Emily told me daisies were your favorite flower." John looked at Emily with an expression she wasn't quite sure of. It wasn't a full smile or a look of regret. She wasn't sure what he was trying to tell her.

Did he understand what she'd been telling him about her mother? Did he finally see how her remarks could cut through her like a knife? Whatever it was, she hoped it was enough for him to understand what she had been trying to tell him all this time. If he didn't find a way to let her go, this would be their future.

Just as Emily was going to suggest they leave, Susie walked through the doorway. "How's it going in here?"

"Fine." Emily smiled. "Do you think you could find a vase for these flowers?" She pointed to the bouquet Dorothy held tight against her chest.

"John brought them for me." Dorothy inhaled the fragrance and smiled.

"I'll see what I can find." Susie replied. "Right now, it's time for Dorothy to have dinner in the dining room with everyone else."

"We were just leaving." Emily moved closer to John and took his arm.

John stood up but not before leaning down closer to Dorothy. "It was so nice to meet you, Mrs. Clayton. I'd like to come back and visit you sometime if that is all right."

"I would like that, John." Dorothy smiled as she inhaled the smell of the flowers again. "Next time maybe you could bring Emily with you instead of that girl." Dorothy pointed in Emily's direction.

Her heart breaking, Emily took John's hand and led him toward the door not saying a word. She didn't want to hear Susie tell her again what a bad day her mother was having. She didn't want to hear it was the disease talking. She didn't want to be here. She wanted to go home. She wanted to curl up in her bed and cry until she couldn't feel the hurt anymore. More than anything she wanted her mother.

****

The ride home was quiet. Emily made small talk when John would ask a question about anything but their visit. Otherwise her focus was on driving. She was thankful he was considerate enough not to touch on the subject of her mother because it was all she could do not to break down in tears. The deep discussion about today would have to wait until she had time to gather her strength back.

She couldn't imagine putting someone she loved through what she went through each time she visited her mother. At first it was sporadic, but now it was every visit. Even on what Susie called her mother's good days, she still didn't recognize her.

John must have noticed from the look on her face how difficult it was for her. Her own mother not even recognizing who she was. Placing her mother in a care facility was the hardest day of Emily's life. She'd been her mother's care giver until she no longer could handle her care.

The day she came home from work and her mother threatened to call the police because she thought a stranger was breaking into her home was fresh in Emily's mind.

She could remember the look of terror in her mother's eyes. She knew then there was nothing more she could do for her. Nothing but love her and hold onto the memories of the good times they'd shared together. The person she placed in the care facility was not her mother. She was who the disease had turned her mother into.

Emily turned to look at John as he stared out the car window. He would never understand what she'd been through and what was possible, if they became closer, he would go through. This disease had not only claimed her mother, it had also claimed Emily's future.

Emily took a deep breath to calm her thoughts. It was up to John now. He saw what it was like for her and she gave him the chance to end things now. All she could do now was pray she could handle whatever he decided, because she could easily fall hard for him. He was everything she wanted, but thought she couldn't have.

CHAPTER FOURTEEN

Samuel Piper

"I'm back, Dad." Piper spoke loudly as he entered his father's house. Walking through the living room and into the kitchen, Piper found his father sitting at the kitchen table staring out the window. His normal place when he was in deep thought. Piper poured a cup of coffee and took a seat at the table with his father. It wouldn't take long before the other deputies in Johnson County tracked him down while he was in town.

"I need to get back to Puckerbrush soon. What was so important I needed to come home?" Piper took a sip of his coffee and waited as his father's expression told him whatever he had to say would be difficult. "Are you all right, Dad? Did the doctor find something when they checked you out? I haven't gotten a call from the doctor. Have you?"

"No. The doctor said I was fine when I saw him. Just old." Robert managed a half smile, his gaze still locked outside.

"Then what is it?" Piper asked, leaning in closer to his father as he waited for any reply. "What did you want to talk about?"

"I need to tell you a story." Robert paused.

"Dad! You called and asked me to come home in the middle of the day to tell me a story?" Piper leaned back in his chair and sighed. Since his mother died, he was the only one his father had to talk to. Piper knew he was lonely and he did all he could to make himself available for his father. It had taken a toll on his personal life, but he knew his father would do the same for him. His father was there for him when he needed him after his mother passed. Piper knew it was his turn to do the same.

Robert took a deep breath. "I promised your grandmother I'd never tell you or anyone else." Robert continued looking through the window as he searched for the right words.

"Dad, you're worrying me. What story? Just say what it is you want to tell me." Piper glanced down at his watch.

Robert turned toward his son finally breaking his gaze from out the window. His expression was solemn and he finally spoke. "Your Grandfather Piper was not my biological father."

"What?" Piper exclaimed. "What are you talking about Dad?"

"When your grandmother became ill, she knew she didn't have much time left. She'd carried this guilt with her all her life. She had the answer to some questions I'd been asking all my life." Robert paused.

"What questions, Dad?" Piper asked. "You're really not making much sense. You wanted me to come home in the middle of the day so you could tell me you had questions about Grandfather Piper?"

"Listen to me, please." Robert's eyes were pleading. "You see, my brothers and sisters all looked like my father. I was the only one who didn't share the shape of his nose or his ears. The Piper ears. All the other children shared those traits, but not me. My mother always said I got her genes. Since I was the first, she gave me all her genes and my Father's got lost in the shuffle. That always made me laugh." Robert looked down at the cup of cold coffee sitting in front of him on the table.

"I remember her saying that." Piper smiled. "It always made me laugh too."

"I wish it was the truth."

"Why wouldn't it be the truth? It sounds logical to me?" Piper asked.

Robert locked his gaze with his son. "My biological father is Edward Dalton."

"Who's Edward Dalton?" Piper waited for his dad to answer. He hoped he would laugh or smile to let him know he was joking around and making up a name. Instead his expression remained solemn. He'd never seen his father with such a serious look.

"Edward Dalton was the traveling evangelist who was Matthew and Emily's biological grandfather."

"You can't be serious Dad." Piper took a deep breath. "Tell me you're joking."

Robert shook his head, "I wish I could." He shifted in his seat, "It was the summer your grandmother and grandfather Piper were going to be married. The traveling evangelist came through Johnson County. Your grandparents, being young and curious, planned to attend. Your grandfather was late picking her up so your grandmother went ahead without him, thinking he would show up when he could."

"Did he show up?" Piper asked tired of waiting for his father to continue the story.

"He didn't. That day your grandfather had been working at the farm and had an accident. Back then there was no way for him to let your grandmother know." Robert paused.

"Why did she go without him. Why didn't she stay home and wait until they could go another night?" Piper questioned.

"Your grandmother was quite strong-willed in her youth and very inquisitive. That night it proved to not be a good combination."

"She went alone to the service. What happened then?" Piper kept asking questions trying to get his father to tell him the complete story. Instead Robert was pausing like he was thinking about what to say next.

"You have to understand it was a church service. She felt completely safe. People from town who she knew and who knew her were there. She had no reason to feel uncomfortable or scared." Robert circled the top of his coffee cup with his finger. "She was going to worship the Lord. What could be safer?"

"I'm guessing it wasn't safe at all." Piper leaned in waiting intently for his father to continue.

"The preacher, Edward Dalton, gave his sermon, then he called everyone who wanted to accept the Lord down to the front of the tent. Your grandmother said when everyone's heads were bowed as they prayed, she looked up and Edward Dalton was smiling at her and motioning her to come down front with the group. He whispered to her he felt the need to pray with her alone. He asked her to meet him after the service."

"And she did?" Piper asked. "Why? Didn't she realize it was a little strange for a preacher to pick one person out of the crowd to pray alone with?"

"Your grandmother was mesmerized by her surroundings. She'd never been out of Johnson Country or to a revival and hadn't met many people who had." Robert paused for a minute trying to gather his thoughts. "Edward Dalton was an oddity and her curiosity got the better of her. I wish I could explain her thinking to you, but unfortunately I don't really understand it myself." A look of confusion showed on Robert's face.

"I wish you could explain it to me also." Piper shook his head as he tried to understand.

"Your grandmother wasn't only curious, she was trusting. She trusted what Edward Dalton told her. She told me he took her back to another tent and he prayed with her. He wanted to know everything about her. He made her feel as if she was special. Then he..." Robert looked down at the table trying to find the strength to say the words.

"You don't have to tell me." Piper reached across the table, placing his hand on his father's arm. "I can fill in the rest of what happened."

After gathering his composure, Robert continued, "She told me she put what happened out of her mind. She never told anyone. She and your grandfather married. Shortly after that, she found out she was pregnant with me. She knew it was too soon for me to belong to your grandfather. She hid the truth from him and waited until it was safe to tell him and he believed I was his."

"Grandmother Piper had lived with this all her life and never told anyone until she told you?" Piper asked.

"Yes." Robert began to weep. "I promised her I would take her secret to my grave."

"And you're telling me now? Why?"

"Emily."

Piper leaned back in his chair and placed his hands on his thighs. "Emily Clayton?"

"I saw a look in your eyes when you introduced me to her. I also saw the hug you gave her. You said she was Matthew's long-lost cousin. I remembered you telling me about her. How her mother was the daughter of a traveling evangelist. I knew I had to tell you. I should've told you when you explained how Matthew found out his father was the son of the traveling evangelist. I knew then you needed to know you were related to Matthew."

"Why didn't you?" Piper asked.

"I couldn't. I knew I didn't want to cause any problems with your friendship. Since you two met, you and Matthew have been close enough to be brothers. People always asked me if you two were brothers. When your grandmother told me her story, I could see the resemblance."

"Why now? Why after you met Emily?"

"I don't know what your relationship with her is. I can't take the chance of you two becoming more than friends. I also could see how much Matthew and Emily wanted to know the name of their grandfather. It might help in their search for other children if there are more."

Piper stopped himself from admitting to his father he considered asking Emily out but something didn't feel right. Maybe it was her interest in John or maybe something or someone was holding him back. He did know he needed to see her and talk to her. He needed to tell her he knew the name of the traveling evangelist. They needed to work together to figure out how they were going to break the news to Matthew. Until they told him, no one else could know. Not even John.

CHAPTER FIFTEEN

"Welcome back." Martha ran toward Abigail and Matthew with open arms. "It's so good to see you two. How was your trip? You two look rested and happy."

"It's good to be home." Abigail gave Martha a hug and watched as Matthew did the same.

"We had a great time." Matthew smiled. "The weather was perfect."

"I'm so happy. We missed you guys while you were gone." Martha smiled.

Abigail waited to ask about Uncle Charles to see if Martha would bring him up in the conversation. He'd decided to stay in Puckerbrush for a while longer instead of returning home after the wedding. He hadn't come out and said so but she knew he was lonely in Chicago. Matthew offered to have him stay at their house while they were on their honeymoon. Uncle Charles happily accepted.

Abigail knew he wanted to stay and spend some more time with Martha so she was happy he took Matthew up on his offer.

"How have things been going here?" Abigail tried to see if Martha would give out any information.

"About like normal. Things quieted down after your wedding." Martha stopped there.

Abigail knew it was going to be up to her to find out any more information. "Has Uncle Charles been coming in for dinner?"

"Oh, yes. He's been here every night since you two left."

"And..." Abigail waited for Martha's reply.

"And, we've had some time to talk and get to know each other. I like your uncle very much." Martha avoided looking at Abigail.

"That's good to hear." Abigail watched Martha's expression. She wasn't good at hiding things. There was something she wasn't telling her.

"I'm sure when you see him, he'll share his news with you." Martha put her hands in her apron pockets.

"News?" Matthew asked.

"What news is that?" Abigail asked.

"I would rather he be the one to tell you." Martha smiled. "I think you're going to be happy."

"You can't leave us hanging, Martha." Abigail exclaimed.

"All I'm going to say is that you might be seeing a lot more of your uncle." Martha turned and started walking back toward the counter. "Would you guys like something while you're here?"

"We did stop in to have lunch, but now I'm not sure if we shouldn't go find Uncle Charles and find out what's going on." Abigail followed Martha to the counter.

"He should be here any time so you can go ahead and order." Martha smiled.

Abigail and Matthew took a seat at the counter looking at each other with a blank stare. The bell on the café door rang and a voice from behind them made both of them turn around.

"Welcome home." Charles walked up behind them and put a hand on each of their shoulders. "It's good to see both of you. How are you two doing? You look well."

"We're doing good." Abigail patted her uncle's hand. "What's this I hear about you having news for us?"

"I guess I do have some news to share with both of you." Charles took a seat next to Abigail at the counter.

"What is it?" Abigail asked as she turned toward her uncle.

"I've decided to move to Puckerbrush." Charles smiled as he glanced in Martha's direction again.

"Move to Puckerbrush!" Abigail grabbed Matthew's knee so hard it made him jump. "That's wonderful, but what made you decide that?"

"I've enjoyed getting to know the people here. Everyone has made me feel so at home. I've never been to a town that made me feel so welcome." Charles paused for a moment. "I decided I wanted to stick around and see what else Puckerbrush has to offer."

"That's a huge decision." Abigail looked at her uncle. "Are you sure about this?"

"I've never been more positive of anything." Charles smiled as he glanced in Martha's direction again.

"You're not telling me everything, Uncle Charles." Abigail took his hand. "Tell me what's really going on."

"The girls are grown and have their own lives. I'm pretty much on my own in Chicago since you parents moved." Charles hesitated for a few seconds then glanced in Martha's direction. "I have a good reason to want to move here and her name is Martha."

"You mean the two of you?" Abigail pointed back and forth between Charles and Martha.

"You sound surprised." Martha smiled. "What are you thinking, Abigail?"

Taking turns looking at the smiles on each of their faces, Abigail replied, "I think it's wonderful. I love the idea." She reached over and hugged her uncle. "I'm so happy for both of you." She jumped up from her seat and ran around the counter and hugged Martha. "You guys are two of my favorite people. Nothing would make me happier than to see you two together."

Matthew reached over and shook Charles' hand. "Welcome to Puckerbrush."

"Thanks, Matthew." Charles smiled.

"Where are you going to live?" Matthew asked. "You're welcome to stay with us as long as you want or need."

Charles laughed. "Thank you for the offer, but I couldn't do that. You two are newlyweds. You don't need another person running around your house. You need your privacy."

"Are you sure?" Matthew asked." There aren't many places here in Puckerbrush to rent."

"I've already talked to Berta and she's going to give me a good rate on a room at the Puckerbrush Motel. I've already been looking for a house. I have a few options." Charles glanced in Abigail's direction. "One of the places is Eldon's farm."

"You're kidding?" Abigail leaned against the counter. "I knew he had a farm, but I've never been there. He didn't have time to show it to me."

"I'm going out to look at it again this afternoon." Charles reached over and took Abigail's hand. "Why don't you come with me? You and Matthew."

"We would love to." Abigail didn't hesitate to accept his offer.

"I'm afraid I have to pass." Matthew held his hands up in the air. "I have to meet with Piper and catch up on all the happenings here in Puckerbrush while we were gone."

"Are you sure you have to do that today?" Abigail asked. "We just got back."

"I know that look." Matthew laughed. "That's your *I want you to do this* look. We may not have been married that long but I learned your looks."

"Please." Abigail asked again.

"I can't. I promised Piper I'd meet with him so he can get back to his regular job." Matthew explained. "I'm sure he wants to get back to Johnson County and relieve the deputy who's filling in for him."

"I'll be happy to go with you, Uncle Charles. I really want to see Eldon's farm." Abigail patted his hand.

"All right then. I was going to have something to eat and then meet the realtor there. You guys want some lunch?" Charles asked.

"We can stay and have some lunch. I'll meet with Piper as soon as we are done." Matthew looked at Martha. "I've been wanting one of your bacon cheeseburgers since we've been gone."

"That sounds really good. I'll take one too." Abigail said.

"Make that three." Charles held three fingers in the air.

"Three cheeseburgers coming up." Martha disappeared into the kitchen.

Abigail took three glasses from behind the counter, filled them with iced tea then placed one in front of Matthew and Charles. "Here you go, guys." She picked up the other glass and took a drink. "It's good to be home."

162

CHAPTER SIXTEEN

Abigail helped Martha clear the dirty dishes from the counter and take them into the kitchen. She prepared a fresh pitcher of tea. Refilling her glass and then starting to refill Matthew's, he put his hand over his glass.

"I've got to get going. Piper's waiting." He stood, wrapped his arms around Abigail's waist and kissed her. "Have fun this afternoon with your uncle. I'll see you at home later. I can't wait to hear all about it."

Abigail smiled and watched Matthew walk out the café door and to the car.

"You guys look happy," Charles replied interrupting her thoughts.

"We are." Abigail smiled thinking back over the past two weeks they had spent together. "Very happy."

"Abigail." Martha called from the kitchen door motioning for her to come there.

"I'm going to check and see if Martha needs anything else. I'll be right back then we can go whenever you're ready" Abigail patted her uncle's shoulder before she made her way to see what Martha wanted. "What's up?"

Martha quietly began to explain. "I wanted to talk to you about John and Emily."

"Oh, yes. I wanted to ask you how things were going but I was so shocked by you and Uncle Charles' news I completely forgot." Abigail leaned in close so she could hear Martha.

"I'm not sure how it's going."

"Haven't they been out a few times?" Abigail asked.

"They have. They spent the night together after your wedding which surprised me. They've seen each other a few times these past weeks. I thought everything was going really well." Martha paused. "I'm not sure now."

"What do you mean? Did John say something?" Abigail was curious to hear what Martha had to say.

"Like I said, she's been here a few times, but one night, before she came for dinner, she met with Piper. John thought they were getting along great until he saw her going into the sheriff's office."

"You don't think something's going on there, do you?" Abigail asked.

"I'm not sure what to think." Martha sighed. "I don't want John to get hurt, but I don't know what to do. I thought maybe you could talk to Matthew and he could talk to Piper and find out."

"I'll ask him to check with Piper when I see him tonight. Who knows, maybe Piper will say something to him this afternoon when they're meeting. Whatever happens, I'll let you know." Abigail leaned her head to the side. "I can't believe Piper would do anything behind John's back. Matthew always talks about how him, Piper, and John hung out together. They've known each other for too long."

"That's what I think." Martha stepped back from the counter. "But John acts like he has a lot on his mind. He's moping around like a lost puppy dog."

"Poor John." Abigail tried not to laugh at the thought of how John must look if that's how Martha described him. "No wonder he hasn't been out here to welcome us home."

"He's probably in the back room licking his wounds."

Abigail could tell by Martha's expression she was worried about him.

"If you two women are through talking, I'm ready to go." Charles interrupted them as he walked up to the kitchen door.

"I'm ready." Abigail turned around. "Let's go check out Eldon's farm." She took her uncle's arm and led him out the door. "We'll talk later, Martha."

Charles turned and blew Martha a kiss before he opened the café door for Abigail. "After you."

****

The loss of Eldon too fresh, and worried about whether she and Matthew were going to make it, Abigail didn't make a trip to his farm after he passed. It was too much for her to process at that time. There was no way she could go through Eldon's belongings.

She knew it was still going to be hard to see where he lived for so many years, but she was ready. She needed to do this. She and Eldon were destined to meet. Their lives were meant to cross. Too many things happened to bring them together to believe otherwise. Her Great Great Aunt Angelica found Eldon when he was abandoned as a child on a dirt road in Puckerbrush. Fate had brought her to Puckerbrush to write an article.

Not only did she find the lost aunt her mother had been looking for, but she also found Matthew. Eldon played a part in all of those happenings. He'd be with her forever.

"We're here." Charles turned into the dirt drive and pulled up close to the house next to the car of th realtor who was waiting for them on the porch.

"It looks just like I thought it would." Abigail smiled as she climbed out of the car. It was almost as if she could see Eldon sitting in the rocker on the wrap-around porch, drinking a cup of coffee and enjoying the sunset. The porch and the plank board siding were painted white and black shutters framed the windows. She brushed a tear away that had made its way down her cheek.

"Good morning." A nicely dressed man moved closer to shake their hands. "I'm Richard Jones. It's nice to see you again, Charles. I see you brought company."

"This is my niece, Abigail Stratford." Charles placed his hand on Abigail's arm.

"Stratford-Thompson." Abigail corrected him.

"You'll have to give me time to get used to calling you that." Charles smiled. "You'll always be a Stratford to me." Charles leaned over and kissed Abigail on the cheek.

"It's nice to meet you, Abigail." Richard Jones smiled. "Stratford-Thompson? You must be Matthew's new wife."

"I am." Abigail beamed with pride.

"I can finally say I know everyone in town now."
Richard Jones laughed. "Let's go take a look at the
house."

Abigail followed behind Richard Jones and her
uncle as they climbed the wood steps leading to the
front porch. It felt solid. The single wooden rocker
placed right outside the front door had been used and
weathered with time. A coffee ring on the left arm of the
rocker almost brought Abigail to tears. It was hard for
her to think of all the years Eldon had spent here alone.
No one to share meals with. No one to watch the sunsets
with. No one to talk to. How she wished she could have
changed that for him.

"I opened up the house so we'd have some fresh
air while we looked around." Richard pulled open the
squeaky screen on the front door. The noise it made as
it opened reminded Abigail of the screen at her
grandmother's. There was something about a front
porch and a squeaking screen door that made her feel
safe. All it needed was a swing.

"Eldon left this house to the Catholic Church when
he passed away. He stipulated in his will the house was
to be sold and the money was to be used for the
children. Eldon was always thinking of the children."
Richard Jones smiled.

Looking around, Abigail didn't have to try and imagine Eldon living there. It was as if he was everywhere. She felt his presence as she touched every piece of well-worn furniture she passed.

"Are you all right?" Charles asked as he glanced at her.

"I'm fine." Abigail managed a smile. "What do you think so far?"

"It's bigger than I imagined. I can see it's been well taken care of. The wood floors are in good shape. The appliances could use a little updating." Charles continued looking around.

"I'm of the understanding that Eldon built this house. After he married, he and his wife moved in and started their family. Of course, you know the rest of the story." Richard's face showed a sadness the entire town must have felt when they thought of Eldon.

"I didn't know he built this house." Abigail began to notice all the special touches Eldon added to make this a home. "Knowing that makes it even more beautiful. I can't wait to see the rest."

"The bedrooms are down this hallway." Richard Jones led the way.

Following behind Richard and Charles, Abigail noticed the walls were bare. There wasn't a picture hanging anywhere. No family photos. No paintings. Nothing in the way of wall decorations at all.

"This would be the master bedroom. I don't know if you would have to use this room as the master. All three bedrooms seem to the same size." Richard explained. "This room does receive more light during the day than the rest. Maybe that's the reason why."

Abigail noticed some frames on the bedside table. She made her way to the bed and sat down on the edge so she could examine each of the photos. One was of a younger Eldon and a woman who looked to be pregnant. Abigail ran her fingers over the dusty glass protecting the photo. The smiles on their faces told her they were happy. She felt the love between the two which made her smile.

The other frame held a picture of a young girl. Abigail imagined she was in her early teens. It had to be Mary, Matthew's biological grandmother. She was beautiful. Abigail could see Eldon in her smile. How hard it must have been for Eldon to lose both of these women. The only two pictures in the entire house summed up Eldon's life.

"What do you think, Abigail?" Charles asked as he sat down next to her on the bed.

She wanted to say how the house reminded her of Eldon. She wanted to tell her uncle to buy the house so she could go through all the memories here and learn more about a man who she'd known for such a short time but had such a huge impact on her life. That was how she felt but her uncle was the one buying the house.

"I think it's perfect for you, but you're the one who has to live here." Abigail patted his knee. "You have to make the decision."

"I would like to put in an offer." Charles smiled at Abigail then stood and moved closer to Richard.

"Let's go back to my office and write an offer and I'll present it to the church." Richard smiled.

"That sounds good." Charles shook Richard's hand.

"Are you ready?" Charles asked Abigail who was lost in thought.

"Yes. I'm right behind you." Abigail stood from the bed and took another look around the room. She hadn't felt this close to Eldon since he passed. A peaceful feeling engulfed her as she walked from the room and through the house. "Bye, Eldon."

CHAPTER SEVENTEEN

"It was like he was there. Every room in the house I could feel his presence." Abigail sat down in her favorite spot on their couch next to Matthew.

"That had to be weird." Matthew scrunched his nose.

"It was weird but nice at the same time. It's hard to explain." Abigail pulled her feet up on the couch making herself more comfortable.

"The strangest part was there were absolutely no pictures or paintings on any of the walls. The only pictures were in a frame beside his bed. They were of his wife and his daughter, Mary."

"I would've like to have seen those." Matthew remarked.

"When Uncle Charles buys the house, I'll ask him for the pictures. I'm sure he doesn't want them. They'll go perfect on the shelf with your other family photos." Abigail pointed to the shelf against the wall. "They'll be a nice addition."

"Speaking of additions." Matthew reached over and rubbed Abigail's growing stomach. "When are we going to let everyone know we're pregnant?"

Leaning back to make her stomach show, Abigail laughed. "We're going to have to tell everyone soon. I don't know how much longer I can hide it. It's been so hard not to say anything to Martha and Berta the times we met about the Puckerbrush museum. It's been an easy pregnancy so far, but I worried one of the smells of food John was cooking in the café would bother me. I've been lucky. I could call Mom and Dad right now. I'm sure they'd be upset if I told anyone before them." Abigail picked up her cell phone from the table in front of them. "After Mom and Dad, we can tell Martha then Berta and the whole town will know before we can take another breath."

"You're right about that." Matthew laughed.

Abigail dialed her phone, put the call on speaker and listened to the ringing.

"Hello." Carol Stratford answered.

"Mom, it's Abigail and Matthew. I have you on speaker. Is Dad nearby?"

"He's right here next to me," Carol replied. "What's going on?"

"Can you put me on speaker. Mathew and I have something to tell you guys." Abigail asked.

"Ok, you're on speaker. What's up?"

"Are you there, Dad?" Abigail waited for her father to answer.

"I'm here sweetheart. How are you?" Daniel Stratford asked.

"Matthew and I are pregnant. You're going to be grandparents." Abigail waited for any reply. There was nothing but silence. "Mom. Dad. Are you guys there?" The only noise that began coming through the phone sounded like sniffles. "Mom, are you crying?"

"Of course." Carol finally answered.

"We're so happy for you guys and I can't believe we're going to be grandparents." Daniel Stratford said. "Your mother's nodding in agreement."

Abigail laughed. "I'm so glad you're happy. Matthew and I wanted you to be the first to know." Abigail could feel her eyes begin to fill with tears. "I'm going to let you go now. I'll give you all the details when we know more."

"I love you guys. I'm so happy." Carol managed to say a few more words before she ended their call.

"Well, that went over good." Matthew smiled as he reached in his pocket and pulled out a quarter. "Now do we flip this coin to see if it's Martha or Berta we tell next?"

****

"I asked Piper and Emily to meet us at the café. They said they'd be here around noon." Matthew turned and looked out the window.

"I'm sure they'll be here soon. I also asked Uncle Charles." Abigail reached over and patted his hand. "You're really excited about telling everyone, aren't you?"

Matthew looked back at her and smiled. "I am. I know everyone's going to be happy and I've kept this a secret for so long. I want to get it out there."

"It hasn't been that long, Matthew. It's only been a few months. I wanted to make sure we got past the first few months and everything was good." Abigail rubbed her hand across her stomach.

"I know but it was so hard to keep it a secret. I wanted to shout it from the roof top." Matthew leaned over and kissed her.

"It's been hard. I know. Now we don't have to keep it a secret. Soon everyone we care about will know." Abigail smiled. "Not to change the subject because I would love to keep talking about our baby, but there's something I wanted to mention to you."

"What's that?"

"Martha told me that John and Emily are getting along fine. They had a good first date and Emily has been to Puckerbrush a few times since then to see John. You heard her say she was enjoying getting to know John. I guess they spent some time together after the wedding."

"That's good." Matthew expression turned to one of questioning. "Isn't it?"

"Yes. It's great, but Martha said when Emily came to town these past weeks, she stopped and met with Piper before she came to see John. Did Piper say anything to you?"

"No. He didn't say anything about Emily. We talked about how things went while we were gone and he caught me up on all the happenings in Puckerbrush which pretty much amounted to nothing." Matthew laughed.

"I guess Emily never mentioned to John she was meeting with Piper. It made John a little uncomfortable when he saw her going into the sheriff's office." Abigail placed her head in her hand. "What do you think she had to talk to Piper about?

"I really don't know." Matthew rubbed the back of his neck. "Maybe they'll say something about it when they get here." Matthew pointed out the window. "They're here now. We'll wait and see what they say."

"They're together in Piper's car." Abigail took Matthew's hand as she watched them climb out of the car. Piper stopped and opened the back door.

"His father's with them." Abigail exclaimed. "What do you think Robert's doing here?"

"I have no clue." Matthew shrugged.

"You know that moment of surprise when I told you we were pregnant?" Abigail smiled at Matthew.

"Yes."

"I think that moment's going to have nothing on what we're going to hear today."

"Not everything that happens in Puckerbrush is a shock or scandal. Maybe his father wanted to come for another visit. He enjoyed meeting everyone at our wedding." Matthew explained.

"Like you said, we'll have to wait and see." Abigail laughed.

"Hi, you two." Piper waved from the front door of the café he held open for Emily and his father to walk through. "I hope you haven't been waiting too long."

"Hi, Emily. It's good to see you again." Matthew stood and greeted her with a quick hug and then gave Piper a quick man hug. "It's good to see you again, Piper."

"It's good to see you, Matthew. Hi Abigail." Emily leaned down and gave her a hug before she took a seat at the table.

Robert Piper didn't say a word as he took a seat next to Emily. Piper made sure his father was seated before he took the chair next to him.

"It's good to see you again, Mr. Piper." Abigail patted the hand he had placed on the table then smiled at Piper.

"You too, dear." Robert tried to manage a smile.

"I hope you're feeling better than you were the last time Matthew and I saw you." She was genuinely concerned.

"I'm feeling much better." Robert attempted a smile once again.

The feeling in the pit of Abigail's stomach told her there was something not right. Robert was holding something back.

"I'm glad you decided to come back to Puckerbrush for a visit." Matthew put his hand on Robert's shoulder then took a seat at the table next to Abigail. He motioned for Martha and John to join the group.

"Sorry I'm late. Looks like I'm the last one to the party." Charles waved as he walked toward the group.

"Hello everyone." Martha and John walked up to the table with Berta following closely behind. Martha was carrying a pitcher of iced tea in one hand and a few glasses in the other. John was behind her with several more glasses. She winked at Charles before she filled each glass with tea and handed them around the table.

Abigail watched as Emily stood and gave John a lingering hug and a huge smile. She poked Matthew's leg under the table hoping he would notice.

Berta made her way around greeting everyone and then took a seat at the end of the table.

"I'm glad you all could join us today. Abigail and I have some news we want to share with you." Matthew paused for a second as Martha audibly gasped. "We're pregnant."

"I knew it." Martha squealed as she held up her clenched fists. "I'm so happy for you two. You're going to have a beautiful baby." After jumping up and down a few times, Martha put her arms around Matthew and Abigail's neck and hugged them both at the same time. "I'm going to be a whatever!" she exclaimed. "I really don't care what I am. I'm just so happy for you guys."

"Thanks, Martha." Abigail did her best to try and return Martha's hug, but she had her arms around her neck so tight she could hardly move.

"I'm so happy for you two!" Berta exclaimed.

"Thank you, Berta." Matthew smiled as he watched her clap her hands in the air.

"That's great news. Congratulations." Piper stood and shook Matthew's hand and gave Abigail a hug when Martha finally let go.

"Congratulations." John and Emily both smiled.

Abigail noticed Robert didn't move a muscle or react in any way to their news. He sat stoic in his chair as everyone else celebrated the news. "We told my parents first. We wanted you all to be the next to hear the news."

"I'm happy for you." Charles shook Matthew's hand and hugged Abigail. "I bet your mother and father were very happy when they heard the news."

"They were." Abigail smiled. "I'm just sorry they're so far away."

"I'm sure they'll come visit often. Now that I'm living here, they can stay with me." Charles smiled.

"They'll love that." Abigail smiled as she noticed the room suddenly became awkwardly quiet. She glanced at Robert Piper who looked very uncomfortable as he twisted his fingers over and over.

"We have some news to share with you also." Piper finally spoke up breaking the silence.

Abigail took a deep breath. She could feel there was something about to be said that was going to change the mood of the room. She put her hand on Matthew's leg bracing herself. She knew he must have the same feeling because he put his hand on top of hers and squeezed.

CHAPTER EIGHTEEN

"You remember at your wedding reception, my father started feeling ill." Piper looked at his father who was still silent.

"Yes." Abigail said. "I asked him earlier if he was feeling better."

"Is everything all right?" Matthew asked.

Piper locked his gaze on his father as if he was waiting for his approval before he continued. "My father's in very good health. He's as strong as a horse the doctors say."

"That's great news. I'm glad they didn't find anything wrong." Abigail glanced around the table at everyone's solemn expressions, especially Emily's.

"That was good news. I was worried about him for a few days until he finally told me what happened." Piper put his hand on his father's shoulder. "You want to tell them, or should I?"

After what seemed an eternity of silence, Robert Piper finally spoke. "I should be the one to tell Matthew. You can fill in the blanks if I leave anything out." Robert placed his hands in his lap. "When you introduced me to Emily, I knew I'd heard her name before." Robert glanced in Emily's direction. "Samuel told me how you and Emily were related and neither one knew."

Abigail flinched when she felt Matthew's hand tighten on hers even harder.

"It seems, Matthew, your father and I are half-brothers. You, Samuel, and Emily are cousins." Robert Piper lowered his head and didn't say another word.

Abigail's heart broke for him. She could see the tears gathering in his eyes. She could feel how hard this was for him to share. Glancing first at Matthew, she could see the color disappear from his face and then at Emily's blank expression.

"Did you know about this?" John asked Emily, finally breaking the silence.

"I didn't until Piper called me and invited me to dinner with him and his father so they could tell me. He asked me to stop and talk to him the next time I came to Puckerbrush so he and I could decide how to tell everyone. We wanted Matthew to be the first to know." Emily brushed away a tear falling down her cheek. "When Abigail and Matthew asked us all to meet, we decided it would be a good time to share."

"That's why she didn't say anything to you, John." Piper explained. "I asked her not to."

"I felt bad keeping this secret from you." Emily turned and looked directly at John. "You understand, don't you?"

"Of course," John replied. "I feel bad now that I thought something was going on between you and Piper."

"We're cousins, man! You and I are friends. I would never!" Piper exclaimed as he sat back in his chair and placed his hands on his thighs.

"I didn't know that." John pulled Emily closer to him. "I'm really sorry."

"Let's get back to the story." Piper turned his attention back to Matthew who hadn't said a word. "What are you thinking?"

"How long have you known, Piper?" Matthew asked.

"My father only told me a few days after your wedding. He went to see the doctor that Monday and he checked out fine. They ran a few tests and they all came back good." Piper sat back in his chair. "After a few more days of him thinking about what happened, he finally broke down and told me so I would leave him alone about his health."

"How long have you known, Mr. Piper?" Matthew asked.

Piper glanced at his father. His head was still lowered. "He promised my grandmother he wouldn't tell anyone. You have to understand why he never said anything before. He was afraid it might cause problems with our friendship. Until he met Emily, he thought he would never have to."

Matthew looked across the table at Robert waiting for his answer.

"My mother told me on her death bed. She'd carried so much guilt all her life. I've only known the truth for a few years. Right before she passed. I didn't feel the need to tell Samuel because I didn't realize there were more children out there. When I met Emily and realized her mother was another child, I knew I'd have to tell you and Samuel. I just didn't know how." Robert still couldn't look directly at anyone.

"It's all right. Keep going. They need to hear the whole story." Piper put his hand on his father's shoulder.

"My father didn't even know I wasn't his child." Robert paused. "Maybe he did down deep, but he never let it show. I didn't resemble him at all. My mother never told him about what happened. She never told him my father was Edward Dalton."

"That was his name?" Matthew interrupted. "Edward Dalton?"

"Yes." Robert answered. "His revival was The Salvation Revival. My mother wrote down his name and other information in a journal and gave it to me before she died. She tried to explain why. I know it had to be hard for her."

"I'm sure it was." Abigail agreed. "I know how hard it was for Eldon to share what he knew for all those years."

"She was ashamed of how she let Edward Dalton convince her with all his lies. How he made her feel she was called by God to fulfill his need." Robert looked directly at Abigail. "He's a horrible man."

"He was a horrible man!" Abigail exclaimed.

Matthew's hand tightened around hers as if he was letting her know not to go there.

"I know it was hard for you to come here today and tell me this." Matthew leaned forward to make sure Robert knew he was serious. "Thank you. I've gained another cousin and I know the name of my...our biological grandfather." Matthew waved his hand between Piper, Emily, and himself. "Not that we can do much since we received our letters."

"Those letters may stop the two of you, but they don't know anything about me. I haven't received a letter so that means I can talk all I want. I can even tell everyone his name and the name of his revival." Piper perked up breaking his silence. "Abigail, can you rebook those interviews?"

Abigail glanced at Matthew then back to Robert. "I'm sure I can. You're sure you want to do this?"

"I'm sure." Piper nodded as he looked at his father. "It's time we all find out the truth about Edward Dalton." Both of them tearing up along with Matthew and Emily. She didn't know what to say or if there was anything she could say. All their lives had just connected in a way none of them expected and for reasons none of them knew.

****

"Why did you stop me earlier today from telling Robert that Edward Dalton was dead?" Abigail asked Matthew as she sat down next to him on their couch.

"I really don't know." Matthew explained. "It was hard enough to deal with the fact Robert has known for a while now and never told Piper and I about it."

"Robert was very brave to come forward now. The story of what happened to Edward Dalton is going to come out eventually." Abigail pulled her feet up underneath her.

"I'm sure it will sooner or later, but Robert was already having a hard time. I didn't think we needed to add more." Matthew put his hand on her knee. "You and I knowing what happened is enough for now. I think we need to focus on finding out how many other relatives we have out there."

"Don't you think it would've made Robert feel just a little bit better if he knew what happened to Edward Dalton? To know he received what he deserved or at least what Eldon felt he deserved. To know Eldon had killed Edward Dalton and buried him in a field somewhere?" Abigail rested her elbow on the back of the couch.

"Maybe, but I know how hard it was for me to find out about my family's past. I didn't feel like we needed to add more to Robert's plate right now. Let him deal with having to tell us the truth about his mother, then we can tell him about preacher." Matthew made quote marks in the air.

"You can't even say his name?" Abigail asked.

"His name doesn't deserve to be spoken unless it has to." Matthew explained.

"It's not like we're going to hang pictures of him up on the walls for everyone to see or add a picture to the family photos on the shelf." Abigail pointed toward the shelves holding the family pictures. "I think you do have to get used to the idea of his name being spoken now and then."

"It wouldn't bother me if I never heard his name again." Matthew stared straight ahead not showing any emotion.

"You've witnessed first-hand how keeping secrets affects the lives of the people keeping them, and those secrets affect innocent people as well." Abigail rubbed her protruding belly. "Don't you want to be honest with your child by telling him the truth? If you can't say his name, that might be a little hard to do."

"I don't want my child to grow up knowing an evil man was in his past who ruined the lives of people without even a second thought and his great-great grandfather took care of that man by murdering him and burying him in an empty field somewhere." Matthew snarled.

Abigail put her feet on the floor and moved closer to Matthew on the couch. "Look at me." She put her hand on his arm waiting until Matthew did as she asked. "You know how keeping his secret made Eldon miserable. Look at what happened to Robert's mother. Do you really want to live your life keeping a secret from your own child? Do you want to wait until you're dying to change the lives of your children forever leaving them with questions only you can answer? The secrets of Puckerbrush need to stop now. From now on, everything needs to be out in the open for all to know and see no matter how painful."

Matthew placed his hand gently on her stomach. "I know you're right. I promise I'll do my best to not keep any secrets from our kids."

"That's all I ask." Abigail placed her hand on his. "Piper's going to take your and Emily's place doing interviews. He's going to talk to some newspapers and Cathy called from the morning show where you and Emily did an interview. She wants to do a follow-up interview. She told me they've received so many emails and questions about you two, they want to cover it again. Piper can do that."

"Wow." Matthew sat back on the couch. "I'm sure the family members who sent Emily and I a cease and desist letter won't like that. I'm sure they'll send a letter to Piper after they catch his interviews. I'm sure whoever they are will be watching."

"We'll worry about that when and if they do." Abigail said. "Until then, we do everything we can to find out what we want to know."

"I was tossing around the idea that maybe Emily and I should push them on their threat to sue us if we keep talking publicly. I thought it would give us a way to find the preacher's name. They'd have to provide that in court." Matthew said. "Until Robert gave us his name, the preacher didn't seem real. Now he has a name and a family out there somewhere who doesn't want us to find out about them."

"Let's take it one step at a time. All of us are going to find out everything we need to know about Edward Dalton." Abigail stood and reached her hand out for Matthew to take. "Now let's make dinner. Me and your child are starving."

CHAPTER NINETEEN

"Are you sure you are ready for this?" Abigail put a hand on Piper's arm hoping to calm him a little.

"I'm as ready as I'll ever be." Piper let out a puff of air between his pursed lips.

"I'll tell you what Abigail told Emily and I. Try not to look at the camera and don't forget to breathe. You're going to do great." Matthew put his hand on the back of Piper's neck.

"I appreciate you guys sticking around to watch. It makes me feel better to know you're here."

"Michelle knows what she's doing. Just answer her questions the best you can and follow her lead. I think they're ready for you." Abigail pointed toward the stage.

She and Matthew watched as Michelle and Piper took a minute to get to know each other, then Piper took a seat. The cameraman began his countdown.

"Welcome to *AM San Angelo*." Michelle looked into the camera and smiled. "A few months back we had two guests on our show who told their story of how they had just learned they were cousins. Emily Clayton and Matthew Thompson were their names. We heard their story of how Emily's mother and Matthew's father were illegitimate children of a traveling evangelist."

After Michelle paused for a few moments to let the studio crowd quiet down, she continued. "Our viewers showed so much interest in their story we asked them to return, but unfortunately after they were on our show, they received cease and desists letters from the family of the traveling evangelist." Michelle paused again as there were audible gasps coming from the studio audience.

"Since Emily and Matthew felt they couldn't return to our show, we received a call and learned they had found another cousin." Michelle pointed to Piper. "I'd like everyone to meet Samuel Piper who is the sheriff of Johnson County."

Piper smiled and nodded toward Michelle not saying a word.

"Can you tell us your story, Samuel?"

"Here we go." Matthew put his arm around Abigail's waist as they waited off stage.

"Sure. I'll give it a shot." Piper smiled. "My grandmother had lived with a secret most of her life. She shared her secret with my father on her death bed, of how a traveling evangelist had raped her the night she attended his revival. My father was a child of that rape. She carried the guilt with her all her life and I guess she felt she needed to tell my father the truth before she died."

"How did your father react to this?" Michelle expression showed her interest in what Piper was sharing.

"Not well. He had a difficult time processing what he learned. I can understand why." Piper rubbed his hand down the legs of his jeans and took a breath.

Abigail could see the concern on Michelle's face as she waited for Samuel to continue.

"You see, she was engaged to my grandfather at the time and they married shortly after that night. She never told anyone what happened. After my father was born, my grandfather raised him with both of them believing they were father and son even though my father didn't look much like his father. My father hadn't planned to tell me what he learned. He wanted the secret to die with him."

"Your father knows he's the child of the traveling evangelist?" Michelle asked.

"Yes. My grandmother confirmed it when she told him her story." Piper rubbed the back of his neck.

"Why did he decide to share this with you and not keep it to himself?"

"Matthew and I have been good friends since we were in the police academy together. Matthew had lost his parents and my mother passed away shortly after we met. My father knew Matthew and felt he didn't need to share this information with either of us when he learned it. We were friends and he didn't want anything to change that. He realized he had to tell us after he met Emily at Matthew and Abigail's engagement party. His fear was Emily and I would become more than friends."

"I can see his need to tell you at that point." Michelle said. "I also understand your father told you the traveling evangelist's name."

"Yes. My grandmother shared the man's name. She told my father his name is Edward Dalton." Piper stopped there looking as if he had finally told the world a huge secret.

"Edward Dalton." Michelle paused and glanced at her notes. "May I ask what you would like to find out about Edward Dalton?"

"Emily, Matthew and I want to know how many more people are out there whose father is Edward Dalton. All we want is to find these people, meet them and finally break the cycle of secrets that have been hidden thanks to Edward Dalton."

Michelle glanced at her stage manager who was motioning to her. "We're almost out of time for this segment. I don't think I could have ended our conversation on any better note." Michelle smiled at Piper and shook his hand. "Thank you so much Samuel Piper for being on our show and sharing your story with all of us. We wish you, Emily, and Matthew luck in finding what it is you want."

Abigail looked at Matthew and nudged him with her elbow. "You can breathe now."

"Are you sure?" Matthew laughed. "I feel like I'm waiting for the floor to drop out from underneath all of us."

"Don't say that. I think it went really well." Abigail nudged him again. "Don't be so negative. Piper did great."

"Did I hear my name?" Piper asked as he walked toward them.

"I was just telling Matthew what a great job I thought you did. You answered all Michelle's questions without any hesitation. She couldn't have asked for anything else." Abigail put her hand on Piper's arm.

"Thanks Abigail. I also thank you two for coming with me. Now I'm ready to go home and forget about Edward Dalton for a while." Piper smiled.

"Let's go then. We've already checked out of the hotel." Abigail put her arm through Matthew and Piper's arms and started leading them out of the studio. "There is one thing we have to do before we head home."

"What's that?" Matthew and Piper both asked in unison.

"I'm starving. We need to find someplace to feed this pregnant woman."

CHAPTER TWENTY

"I'm so happy all of you could make it today." Abigail glanced around at everyone seated at the table chatting and laughing as if they hadn't seen each other in weeks. "Matthew and I wanted to make our first Thanksgiving together in our house a special one before the baby comes and our lives turn upside down." Abigail stood and spun sideways so the entire table could see her protruding belly.

Matthew smiled and winked from the other end of the table.

"We couldn't think of a better way than to have all of you join us. Before everyone begins eating, I want to thank Martha who made most of the meal and dessert. With John's expert help and guidance, Matthew and I managed to make the turkey and dressing." Abigail took a seat.

"Thank you two for inviting us to your lovely home and making us all feel welcome. You've done such a wonderful job with the table. It's absolutely beautiful." Berta nodded at Abigail. "Since it's Thanksgiving can I suggest we go around the table and everyone tell something they are thankful for? It's a tradition my family has had since I was a little girl."

"That's a wonderful idea." Martha agreed. "Why don't you start, Berta?"

"All right." Berta cleared her throat and sat up in her chair. "I'm very thankful for all of you. I've always felt like I belonged in Puckerbrush, but since Abigail came here it seems we've all become a close family."

"That's so true, Berta." Martha, sitting next to her, patted her hand. "I'm next so what I'm thankful for has to do with Abigail also. If it wasn't for her, I would have never met Charles."

Charles, sitting next to Martha, leaned over and kissed her cheek. "I'm next. What I'm thankful for also has to do with Abigail. If she hadn't promised me when she was a very little girl that I could be the one to perform her wedding ceremony, I would have never met Martha."

"I'm next, I guess." Matthew leaned back in his chair. "What I'm thankful for also has to do with Abigail. If she hadn't taken the assignment to write an article on Puckerbrush's Centennial Celebration, we wouldn't have met. Also, if I hadn't come to my senses and said 'Puckerbrush' that day on my deck, I'd hate to think where I would be. Since she was willing to stay and help me through what I had learned about my past, I'm now happily married and am going to be a father. I love you." Matthew winked at her again from the opposite end of the table as he watched her wipe a tear away.

"I don't know if I can top that." John laughed along with everyone else. "Here goes. What I'm thankful for also is because of Abigail. If she hadn't discovered the secret of Puckerbrush that had been hiding for years, Matthew would've never tried to discover his past and I would've never met Emily." John leaned over and kissed Emily's cheek.

"That means I'm next." Emily took a quick look around at the people at the table. "What I'm thankful for is definitely because of Abigail. I've found some of the best people in the world I can now call friends. What I've learned since the first day I showed up in Puckerbrush is that if it hadn't been for Abigail, we wouldn't all be here today. I can't think of any place I would rather be." Emily looked at John who had a disappointed expression. "Oh, and of course, I'm thankful for John. I couldn't forget you." She returned his kiss which made him smile.

"I'm up." Piper laced his fingers in front of him. "What I'm thankful for also is because of Abigail. She's the one who started this whole adventure and because of her I have two new cousins. Oh, and since she's managed to find the perfect partner for Martha and John, I'm hoping she'll work her magic for Berta and I."

"Hey!" Berta exclaimed. "I'm happy with my life just like it is."

"Fine. Then Abigail, only work your magic for me. Berta's happy just like she is." Piper laughed along with everyone else.

"What about you, Mr. Piper?" Abigail put her hand on his arm.

"I'm thankful for..." Robert Piper paused and looked around the table. "I'm thankful for the happiness all of you have brought into my life and also Samuel's life. I look around the table and I see family. I also want Samuel to have what you and Matthew have." Robert smiled at Abigail. "I know he will if he has such wonderful people like all of you in his life. Also, Berta, don't give up on sharing your life with someone. It's a wonderful thing."

Abigail caught the smile Robert gave Berta. Since she had met Robert, she could count on one hand how many times she had seen him smile. She liked what she saw.

"It looks like it's my turn." Abigail took a drink of water before she began. "First I have to say, I love you all and what everyone said touched my heart." She placed her hand over her heart. "I thought I had a wonderful life before I came to Puckerbrush, but little did I know what was in front of me. Every one of you are family to me and I'm thankful for each and every one of you." Abigail's voice began to break. She glanced at Matthew and he winked at her.

"Charles has agreed to carve the turkey. If you guys want to start passing the sides, we can all eat." Matthew handed Charles the carving knife and a fork. "Save me a leg."

****

"Oh no you don't." Martha took the plate out of Abigail's hand." You go sit down and put your feet up."

"You won't get an argument out of me." Abigail handed her plate to Martha and took a seat on the couch in the living room turning so she had a view of everyone helping clear the table and talking as they worked. She took out her phone and began taking pictures. She had snuck a few between tears when everyone was going around the table taking turns telling what they were thankful for. This was a Thanksgiving she didn't want to forget.

Eldon kept popping into her mind. How he would have loved to have spent the day with all of them. He probably wouldn't have much to say, but he would have taken it all in and enjoyed every minute. How she would love for him to have lived long enough to be here when the baby was born. This baby would have been the fourth generation. It would have made him so proud. All the hurt and pain he had lived through would have been healed when he laid eyes on this child. She made a mental note of talking to Matthew about deciding on a name for their baby.

Piper took a seat next to her on the couch. "You look deep in thought."

"I was just enjoying watching all of you guys bustling around." Abigail adjusted the way she was sitting. It was beginning to be uncomfortable to stay in one place too long. The baby seemed to like to move and put pressure on different parts of her body.

"I forgot to tell you guys I received my cease and desist letter last week." Piper leaned forward placing his elbows on his knees. "It seems like we hit a nerve with my interview and the article you did in *Ancestry Journal Magazine.*

"Really. Did you hear that Matthew and Emily?" Abigail called.

"Yes." Both answered in unison.

"I've been meaning to talk to all of you about that. I'm glad you brought it up Samuel." Robert Piper took a seat in one of the living room chairs and motioned to everyone else. "If the rest of you want to join us."

Matthew and Emily took a seat on the floor in front of the couch. Berta, Martha, Charles, and John stopped cleaning in the kitchen to listen.

"I know how hard you guys have been working to find more people who can be traced back to Edward Dalton." Robert said.

"We have been, but we're not having much luck." Matthew interrupted. "It seems the family, whoever they are, don't want us to know much more."

"I had an idea and I wanted to ask all of you what you thought. What if we hired a specialist to do tracing?" Robert paused as he waited for a response.

"You mean a genealogist? That would be great but it would cost a lot of money." Abigail said. "Right now, Matthew and I are saving all we can for the baby."

"I've thought about it and Abigail's right, it would cost a lot of money." Emily glanced at Abigail and nodded.

"What if I'm willing to give a sample for DNA tracing and also pay for the genealogist?" Robert asked.

"Dad, you really want to do that? I don't know how much it will cost, but I'm sure it's not cheap." Piper asked.

"Piper's right. It could cost thousands." Matthew said.

"I want to do this. I want all of you and me to know exactly where we came from. If you guys are willing to help me find the right person, I think it's time to put the secrets of Edward Dalton to rest." Samuel glanced around at everyone's faces.

"Come on you guys. Take him up on it." Berta said from the kitchen.

"I agree. If Robert's willing to pay for it, you can't say no." Martha added her opinion.

"I agree." John said.

"If you really want to do this, Mr. Piper..." Matthew looked at Abigail, Piper, and Emily. "Then I don't see how we can say no."

"It's a deal then." Robert slapped his knee with his hand. "We start looking for a genealogist Monday morning."

CHAPTER TWENTY-ONE

A few months later

"You look beautiful, both of you." Abigail put her hand on her growing stomach as she smiled at Martha and Emily. Martha's soft peach colored dress accentuated her figure, tighter at the waist and shorter to show her beautiful legs. Emily's white dress was longer with spaghetti straps and a high bodice and hung loosely around her nice figure. "Those dresses are perfect for both of you."

"Thanks, Abigail." Martha smiled.

"Oh, I got to meet Michael." Abigail reached over and took Martha's hand. "He's just as handsome as John."

"He surprised John and I last night by just showing up at the café. It was so good to see him and be able to give him a hug."

Abigail could see how proud Martha was of both her sons by the ear-to-ear smile on her face. "You two had to be excited."

"Yes, we were so excited. He said he's just here for the wedding though and then has to go back." Martha shrugged. "I'll take whatever time I can get. It's been awhile since we've seen him. Between his job, the kid's school schedule and John and I running the café, it's hard for any of us to get away."

"It's too bad the rest of the family couldn't have come with him." Emily said. "I would have loved to have met them."

"Michael promised he would try to bring the entire family back around Christmas or after the first of the year." Martha held up her hand with her fingers crossed.

"Well, you two women look beautiful and you have two handsome men waiting to marry you." Abigail reminded them.

"I can't believe I'm getting married today." Martha laughed. "I didn't think this would ever happen again and to share the day with my beautiful soon-to-be daughter-in-law."

Emily took Martha's hand. "I couldn't imagine anything that would make me happier. You've been so accepting of me. You've no idea how much that means to both John and I."

"I know you two had differences you had to work through, and I'm so glad you did. You were meant for John. You make him so happy. As a mother, that's all we want for our children." Martha wiped away a tear that began to fall down her cheek.

"You're going to make me cry." Emily said.

"I have a question for both of you." Abigail interrupted the two women before they both ruined the makeup Berta had worked so hard to make perfect. "Are you sure you want me walking down the aisle before you? Abigail turned sideways then ran her hand down her protruding stomach. "Finding a maternity dress for a bridesmaid was next to impossible." She pulled the side of her dress away from her body. "I had to go with this simple floral print."

"You look beautiful." Martha exclaimed. "Of course, we want you and little Matthew to be part of our wedding. Right, Emily?"

"Yes, we do." Emily agreed.

"I feel like a beached whale." Abigail laughed. "You know I could have this baby any day. It might happen when I'm walking down the aisle."

"Just hold it until the we say 'I do' and everything will be fine." Martha laughed.

"I'll try." Abigail took a deep breath and smiled.

"They're ready for the brides." Berta interrupted as she burst into the small room off the chapel putting her hands on her hips as she looked at both brides. "Don't tell me you two have been crying. You're going to ruin your makeup." Berta moved closer to both of the women inspecting their faces. "You both still look as beautiful as when I left you. Now, grab your bouquets and let's get you two married." Berta clapped her hands together like a small child. "Let's go."

Abigail took Martha and Emily's hands as they made their way toward the chapel. Michael was waiting at the doorway of the chapel. Abigail teared up as she heard Martha gasp.

"I thought I would walk you two ladies down the aisle if that's all right with you." Michael held out both his arms. One for his mother and one for Emily.

"We would love that." Emily answered for both she and Martha as they each took an arm.

Abigail took her place in front of the doorway, Michael, Martha, and Emily standing behind her. The music began to play which was Abigail's signal to begin walking down the aisle. Before she took her first step, a small twinge ran across her stomach. She took a deep breath doing her best to ignore it and then began to walk.

Michael, Martha, and Emily followed behind, bouquets in one hand and holding on to Michael's arm with the other hand, smiling at the men who waited for them at the altar. Charles looked handsome in his black three-piece suit, John in his more casual navy-blue jacket, white shirt and tie. Both wearing huge smiles as they watched the two women make their way down the aisle.

Matthew was standing in the best man's place in his dress uniform and Piper, also in his dress uniform was ready to perform the ceremony.

Abigail took her place on the right side of the brides. Matthew, on the left of the grooms, winked at her. Another twinge made her stomach tighten. Taking another deep breath, she managed a smile, hoping Matthew hadn't noticed.

Michael took a seat next to Berta in the front row. Martha took Charles' hand; Emily took John's as they stood between the two men. Piper began the ceremony. Abigail did her best not to focus on the twinges in her belly which were getting stronger and stronger each time.

"We're now to the part of the ceremony where everyone holds their breath." Piper laughed. "If anyone here knows why these couples should not be joined in holy matrimony, let them speak now or forever hold their peace."

A loud moan broke the silence of the chapel. Everyone turned to look at Abigail who was bent over, her hand on her belly. Matthew rushed to her side.

"Are you all right?" He put his arms around her, holding on until she stopped moaning.

"I think I'm in labor." Abigail explained between pants. "I'm so sorry guys."

"Let's get you to the hospital." Matthew insisted.

"What about the wedding. I don't want to miss it." Abigail began to moan again.

"I don't think the baby wants to cooperate." Matthew laughed. "Martha can you stay with her while I go get the truck?"

"Sure." Martha helped Abigail to the closest chair. "Sit down here." Berta hurried over and sat down next to Abigail.

"I'm so sorry, Martha. I don't want to ruin your wedding." Abigail began to cry.

"You're not ruining my wedding. It's fine. Besides it gives your Uncle Charles and John time to make sure this is what they really want." Martha laughed as she looked at Charles and smiled.

"Can you finish without Matthew and I?" Abigail asked.

"We'll be fine. You need to worry about you and little Matthew. I can't wait to meet him." Martha kissed Abigail on the forehead. "He's going to be born on my wedding day. This'll be a very special day for all of us."

Abigail leaned her head on Martha's shoulder and began to moan again. She felt Berta take her hand.

"Let us know when this one stops." Piper leaned down in front her. "Martha, Berta, and I will make sure you get to the front door and help Matthew get you in the truck."

Abigail began to laugh. "You might need to bring the rest of the wedding party to help you lift me in."

"This one must have stopped. Her sense of humor is back." Martha nodded for Piper to help her hold on to Abigail as they made their way to the front door.

Matthew was pulling up in his truck just as they reached the front door. He opened the passenger door as Martha and Piper walked her to the truck. He took her arm and helped her climb into the cab.

"We'll see you at the hospital later." Martha waved at Abigail as Matthew closed the door. "Take care of her."

Matthew nodded in agreement as he ran around the truck and climbed in behind the wheel.

Piper put his arm around Martha's waist. "Let's go get you married."

CHAPTER TWENTY-TWO

"You have a healthy baby boy. He checked out perfectly when I saw him in the nursery earlier. You have something very beautiful to show for probably the hardest eight hours you've ever had. I hope you got some rest last night."

An exhausted but radiant Abigail squeezed Matthew's hand as they both smiled at the bundle of joy snuggled up against her chest. "I did. Thank you, Dr. Smith."

"If you need anything or have any questions, just let your nurse know. I'll check in on you again tomorrow before you leave." Dr. Smith reached into the pocket of her smock and handed Matthew a card. "You can call my office and make an appointment in about a week so we can see how baby's coming along." She placed her hand on top of the baby's head.

"Am I interrupting anything?" Piper asked as he stood in the hospital room doorway.

"No, not at all." Matthew motioned for Piper to come in the room as he stood and shook his hand. "We were just talking to our pediatrician."

"I can wait outside until you guys finish." Piper motioned toward the doorway.

"I was just leaving." Dr. Smith glanced at Piper with a questioning look on her face.

Piper noticed her lingering stare. "I'm Samuel Piper. I'm a friend of the lucky parents." He put out his hand for her to shake.

"Samuel Piper, huh?" Dr. Smith smiled. "Dr. Regina Smith."

Piper stepped back to take another look at her. Her curly brown hair hanging past her shoulders. The sparkle in her green eyes was familiar. "Reggie?"

"Piper?" Dr. Smith asked.

"You two know each other?" Matthew laughed.

"Yes, we do." A huge smile crossed Piper's face. "Reggie here broke my heart."

"Really?" Abigail asked as she waited to hear more of their story.

"I don't remember it that way." Regina laughed. "I seem to remember you broke up with me when I left for college."

Piper rubbed the back of his neck as he tilted his head and smiled. "We're going to have to agree to disagree. What brought you back to Puckerbrush?"

"I wanted to be closer to my family. I decided to start my own practice here in Puckerbrush. My family isn't that far away." Regina explained.

"I'm sure your family likes that idea. I remember how close you guys were." Piper said. "Your father always made sure I brought you home on time. I was scared to death of him."

"He's not so scary anymore." Regina smiled. "What are you doing here in Puckerbrush, Piper?"

"I don't live in Puckerbrush. I still live in Johnson County. I'm the sheriff."

"How do you know the Thompsons?" Regina asked.

"Matthew and I are friends. We met at the academy and have been friends since. Abigail's not so bad either." Piper smiled and winked at Abigail as Matthew patted him on the back giving his approval of his comment.

"Thanks a lot, Piper. I love you too." Abigail shook her head.

"Are Abigail and your wife friends also?" Regina asked.

"I'm not married," Piper was quick to reply. "What about you?"

"Me either." Regina shook her head. "I've been really busy with my career."

"You never found anyone to take my place, huh?" Piper laughed.

"There's that sense of humor I remember." Regina shook her finger at Piper. "I'm going to go. I have another new patient to visit before I leave. It was good to see you Piper."

"You too, Reggie." Piper smiled. "Maybe we can find some time to catch up."

"I'd like that." Regina took another card and a pen from her smock pocket and wrote on the back then handed it to Piper. "Here's my cell. Call me and we'll find a time."

Abigail watched as Piper took the card from Regina. The smile on his face was one she had never seen before. She loved the Piper she had gotten to know but he never showed much emotion. This was a new Piper and she liked this one much better.

Martha, Charles, John, Emily, and Berta walked through the hospital room door as Regina left.

"Do you feel like visitors?" Martha asked as she bent over Abigail and kissed her forehead and sneaked a peek at the baby. "Oh, he's beautiful."

"Yes, he's adorable." Berta squealed as she peeked at the baby over Martha's shoulder.

"Congratulations. How are you feeling, Abigail?" Charles asked as he shook Matthew's hand.

"I'm good, Uncle Charles."

"I talked to your mother and father and they're so excited to meet their grandson. They're making their way here as soon as they can. They wanted me to tell you how much they love you. Of course, your mother was in tears the entire conversation." Charles laughed as he leaned over the bed and gave Abigail a kiss.

"I can't believe you guys took time to come visit. All of you should be off enjoying yourself somewhere sunny and warm. You are married right?" Abigail took turns looking at Martha, Charles, Emily, and John.

"Yes, we are." Martha and Emily replied in unison both holding up their left hands to show off their wedding rings.

"And Berta, I thought you would be resting after all the work you did for the wedding and the Puckerbrush museum."

"I can always rest." Berta explained. "It's not every day I get to see the newest person in Puckerbrush. Also, we decided to delay the opening of the museum a few weeks. Until you get back on your feet and can join us."

"And we couldn't go anywhere without checking on you and the baby first." John smiled.

"John's right. We had to come meet the baby and make sure you were doing all right." Emily smiled. "Can we see him?"

"Yes." Abigail handed the baby to Martha so she could take him closer to John, Emily, and Berta. Charles joined the others. Abigail smiled as she watched all five of them smile, make faces and talk baby talk. It made her happy to see the people who were going to be influential in his life enjoying time with him.

"Have you guys decided on a name yet?" Emily asked as wrapped her fingers around the baby's small hand.

"Oh yeah. What's this little guy's name?" Martha asked.

Matthew looked at Abigail to see if she agreed to share the name they'd decided on.

Abigail smiled and nodded her head.

"Archer Eldon Thompson." Matthew said proudly. "Archer for my father..." Matthew paused. "Eldon for Eldon."

"That's a perfect name." Martha smiled as a tear escaped down her cheek.

"I think so." Abigail agreed.

"You want to hold him?" Martha asked as she looked at Emily and John.

"I would love to." Emily carefully reached over and took the baby from Martha and snuggled him close. Abigail remembered having children was one of the issues Emily and John had to work out. It looked to her as if they'd come to an agreement or if they hadn't, little Archer might be changing Emily's mind.

"I'm going to get going." Piper shook Matthew's hand again and leaned down and gave Abigail a quick kiss. "You guys did good."

"Thank you, Piper. Tell your father hello for us." Abigail asked. "And make sure you let us know when you and Dr. Smith find that time to catch up."

Matthew laughed. "You know you're going to have to fill her in on every little detail. The writer in her is showing up."

"What's this?" Martha asked. "Dr. Smith?"

"Did you see the pretty doctor walking out of the door when you guys were coming in?" Abigail asked.

"Yes. What about her?" Martha asked.

"It seems Piper and Dr. Smith, who's Archer's new pediatrician, know each other. In fact, they go back to high school." Abigail smiled as she looked at Piper to add more to the story.

"I know her as Reggie. We dated in high school." Piper held his hands up in the air. "We broke up when she went to college. Long distance relationships don't work out well."

"It seems they're both still single." Abigail added. "They're going to get together and catch up." She made quote marks in the air with her fingers.

Matthew and Emily looked at each other and smiled. They both made their way to Piper's sides.

Emily nodded at Matthew as if to tell him to go ahead and say what they were both thinking.

"Let me give you some advice. Make sure you know where she was born, if either of her parents were adopted. Let's hope her name doesn't show up when the genealogist finishes our family tracing. If I were you, I'd have her take a DNA test just to be sure there's no Dalton in her family tree."

The room filled with laughter. It was a subject which had brought everyone in this room together. It was a subject of tears, growth, and heartache for everyone here. But now, because of time and forgiveness, it was a subject they could all laugh about now and in the future.

C. DEANNE ROWE

C. Deanne Rowe was born and raised in southwest Oklahoma. She has also lived in Nebraska, Texas, and California. Iowa has been her home for over thirty years where she lives with her husband, two children and their spouses, five grandchildren, and her hero teacup toy poodle, Allie.

She has always loved writing poetry and short stories and became a published romance author later in life. She has published eight books of her own, three in her *Valley* series, four in her *Cowboy Temptation* series and one non-fiction. As one of the Stiletto Girls with Magnolia 'Maggie' Rivers and Glenna West, she is an author of ten novellas in the *Stiletto Girls* series.

You can find additional information about her other writing on her websites:

www.comfortedfromheaven.com

www.cdeannerowe.com

www.thestilettogirls.com

www.ingramcontent.com/pod-product-compliance
Lightning Source LLC
Chambersburg PA
CBHW071504170626
46811CB00007B/2737